Three Broke Moms
Detective Agency

Shay Lawless

Three Broke Moms Detective Agency—Copyright © 2026 by Shay Lawless

ISBN-978-1-940087-78-8

21 Crows Dusk to Dawn
Publishing, 21 Crows, LLC

Shay Lawless

Chapter −1

It was early Wednesday morning when a knock shattered the predawn hush and changed my world entirely. I blinked awake, heart stuttering, certain I'd imagined it.

Then—*rap, rap, rap*—it came again. Louder this time, insistent enough to raise goosebumps on my arms.

My heart slammed against my ribs. The clock glowed 3:11 a.m.—no one decent knocked at this hour unless they wore a badge or meant trouble.

I snapped out of bed and crept down the stairs in stocking feet, wearing an old T-shirt and scruffy green pajama pants printed with faded four-leaf clovers—shabby chic only if you squinted and ignored the decade of wear.

I grabbed my trusty baseball bat from the corner, knuckles whitening around the handle, and peered into the early-fall darkness. But not before flattening my frizzy ginger-copper hair, because if I was about to be robbed, I could at least try not to look my worst. A flash in the foyer mirror showed it was hopeless; in my green pajamas, I looked like a green-eyed Leprechaun who'd lost his hat and his luck.

Under the jaundiced porch light—moths and beetles battering the glass—I made out the blurred blue of police jackets. Two officers. One cradled a bundled child. Two more waited in shadow, shifting from foot to foot.

Pinehaven, North Carolina sits far enough inland that you don't see the ocean, but close enough to smell it on certain mornings. Salt creeps into everything here—metal, wood, memory.

It isn't a tourist town. People pass through Pinehaven on their way somewhere better. Those who stay learn quickly that the town remembers who belongs... and who disappears. But it doesn't stop me from opening the doors wide without peering through the peephole.

"Mommy?" Annie's voice was a whisper, trembling at the edge of the dark. "Is somebody at the door?"

I jumped—I hadn't heard the soft patter of bare feet behind me. My five-year-old, Annie, stood at the bottom of the stairs, clutching her ragged Teddy bear, eyes wide and sleep-fogged.

Annie. Short for Anastasia—a name I once swore would never be shortened, picturing a future of ballet recitals and sparkly tiaras. Two weeks of colic, dirty diapers, and nights screaming into my pillow cured me of that illusion. Annie she became.

Not that it mattered. Annie preferred muddy jeans and baseball mitts to pink tutus—her idea of a recital involved slinging mud at anyone in range.

Her strawberry-blonde hair stuck up in wild tufts, catching the hallway light like a dandelion gone to seed.

"Yes, sweetheart." I kept my voice low and steady. "Go on back upstairs for me, okay?"

"Why?" she persisted, chin jutting out with that stubborn tilt I knew too well.

Of course. Five-year-olds: relentless question machines, all logic and no off switch.

"Because I don't know who's at the door," I said, gently herding her up the first few steps, deflecting the battering ram of why with practiced mom-judo. I waited until her small feet disappeared, then turned back to the door.

I opened the door and a gust of damp, leaf-mulch air slipped inside, raising goosebumps along my arms.

"You're Misty Dawn Bailey?"

I nodded, squinting at the figures. That's when I recognized Shane—Jay's oldest, one of his three kids from his first marriage. Jay, an old boyfriend.

He'd shot up at least two inches since I'd seen him, stretched thin with the raw awkwardness of fifteen. At twelve, when Jay and I split, he'd been all elbows, glasses, and stammered hellos.

Now, his face caught the porch light—no glasses. He looked pale, older than he should, shadows pooling under his eyes.

Fifteen now—was that right?

"The boy here asked if they could stay with you," the officer said, his breath fogging in the porch light. "We checked—you're the emergency guardian. Jay Hensley listed you in case of emergency."

Surprise didn't even come close.

In all fairness, I'd signed forms from Jay's lawyer—assuming they were for routine school permissions or medical decisions when Jay traveled. My heart lurched. I stood there, frozen, while memories from our three years together tumbled through my head. Most painted me not as a partner, but as a glorified babysitter with a side of heartbreak.

"Something..." My voice snagged. "Something happened to him?" Something had.

Jay vanished in early June—depending on who you asked. That's when he stopped answering calls and never came back.

Shane and his sisters lived as if he were still out there somewhere—late, busy, coming back eventually. No one had said the word *gone*. Not out loud. Molly, thirteen and a half, mostly played mommy as best as she could. Then school started. Six-year-old Daisy got into a fight, the principal called, and whatever they'd been holding together unraveled. They couldn't hide it anymore.

Now, they were on my porch—and minutes later, inside my hand-me-down brick two-story at the edge of town. I caught my nosy neighbor Edna Jefferson peering out her window before I shut the door behind us. I imagined she was already on the phone, telling the women in her book club there was something going on at my house.

And it involved the police.

Two days later—after a stretch of meals, forms, and too-little sleep—Marty Fields—part-time officer—filled in the rest. She was part-time police now, but we'd known each other since kindergarten, and she'd worked the same desk job with me when I tried my hand at law enforcement. Jay's parents were gone—his mother dead, his father estranged—and the kids' mother had signed away her rights years ago. No one else was close, stable, or willing to answer a knock at 3 a.m.

That night, when the house finally quieted, I stood in the hallway listening to unfamiliar breathing—counting it the way I used to count Annie's as a baby, just to make sure nothing slipped away while I wasn't looking. In the days that followed, I learned three things: the kids didn't sleep, Annie didn't stop circling them like a guard dog, and Pinehaven noticed everything.

Everyone in town knew me as steady and sensible—the

woman you trusted with keys and kids. But that wasn't the version I listened to in the dark. Jay was the only one who'd glimpsed the other side, the one who panicked when things went bad. Now, I couldn't stop wondering if leaving the kids with me was a warning—something Jay set in motion because he knew things were already unraveling, and if I read the signs right, maybe he was already gone for good.

Somewhere outside, a dog barked—sharp and frantic, the kind of sound that makes your scalp tingle. A floorboard groaned underfoot, echoing up the hallway, a reminder that nothing was normal anymore. The question pressed, hot and heavy, against my ribs: What had Jay gotten himself into—and why had he left me to deal with it?

Chapter –2

"Big Ed's Surveillance Services. No job's too big, no job's too small—especially if that pretty wife of yours just dropped the ball."

My voice echoed across the kitchen as I cradled the landline, shifting an armful of sour-smelling laundry from hip to hip. I was wearing my frumpy overall jeans and a worn T-shirt—the uniform Pinehaven expects from me. Functional. Forgettable.

I caught my reflection in the darkened pantry door and paused anyway. I always do.

If I'm going somewhere with a purpose—asking questions, listening more than I talk—I dress for it. Not undercover exactly. Just intentional. Clothes change how people answer you. How long they linger. What they assume you already know. Today didn't call for that. Today I needed to look like everybody else. And sometimes that's the best disguise.

Yikes, though. Who knew three kids could generate so many clothes in just two days after they came through my door? And it's not like they'd been running laps—Shane, Molly, and Daisy mostly huddled on my couch, eyes glazed, the TV throwing blue shadows across their faces. I'd planned to give them time to settle, but the deeper their silence sank in, the more certain I became: school starts tomorrow.

By then, the week had already blurred together. Everything after that felt like one long lead-up to morning—laundry, phone calls, paperwork, and the quiet pressure of knowing the clock was already ticking.

Besides, three mornings a week—ten to noon— Wally Singer, the private investigator I work for, insists I show up for a self-defense class at the old elementary school, now the Paul Finnigan Community Building. Nonnegotiable. He says he needs it for his insurance.

Miss a day and I make it up on Saturday. That's when Tina Metzger must come in just for me.

Tina runs the program. Former world title holder. She says "sparring," but what she really does is remind me, efficiently and without apology, that confidence doesn't count for much once someone gets their hands on you. I limp home afterward, sore and humbled, which I suppose is the point.

"Big Ed's—" I repeat after a pause. I should've said *spouse*. "How can I help you?"

A woman—maybe the sixth this month—wanted a private investigator to tail a husband she suspected had swapped her for someone younger. Big Ed loves those calls. Big Ed—whose real name is Wally Singer—calls it *easy money*: Follow the man. Snap the photos. Collect the check.

He collects the check. I do the trailing.

Wally is sixty-something, weathered like an old wind vane rusted and stuck to a roof. He was bald now. He used to wear a toupee, but with all the nervous hand-runnings through his hair, it kept shifting and sliding until one day it just... didn't make it back on. He gave up after that.

These days he reminded me of the St. Francis statue my mom keeps in her garden—hair forming a dark, uneven halo around his head, jowly hound-dog cheeks, bloodshot eyes that always looked like they'd seen too much and slept too little.

He favored cheap suits with a used-car-salesman vibe, the middle button always undone to make room for a soft belly he pretended wasn't there.

Doing the trench work isn't that fun. Despite what people think, it isn't glamorous, not like TV. It's hours parked in a stale car, watching the same two battered sedans in the corner of some cracked lot, fumbling a camera with cold, numb fingers, trying not to get caught snapping useless photos through smeared glass. Digging receipts out of garbage. Endless phone calls pretending I'm someone else. Mostly thankless tasks.

But every penny matters when you're raising kids solo— juggling groceries, a car payment, and a mortgage— pretending it doesn't scare you half to death.

When I hung up, I was elbow-deep in the washer, stuffing clothes tight so I wouldn't waste detergent. Or time. Three loads left, payday a week away—assuming nothing snapped or ran out first. And I had to be at a job in twenty minutes.

The phone shrilled again, slicing through the laundry's hush. A familiar laugh crackled on the line. "You know I only called to hear you deliver that stupid line, right?"

"Screw off, Ryder." Noah Ryder—everyone called him by his last name. I'd known that face since grade school: tall, broad-shouldered, just buff enough to lord it over the rest of us. His ego had muscle, too.

Like me, he bounced around local jobs after college—police station, fire department, county office, township garage. I stuck with the police, briefly. He went fire department.

"Heard you're officially outnumbered now," he drawled,

and I could picture the smirk. "So much for sleeping in and doing whatever you want, huh?"

"Fall through any burning floors lately?" I shot back, aiming for playful, but the edge slipped in anyway.

He went silent.

Yeah. Too far. His fire department career lasted a year longer than my police stint, but mine ended with Annie. His ended when he dropped two stories in a burning apartment, trying to rescue one of his best friends, Billy Ramsey. Heroic. Mine? Just a small-town punchline.

I was oversensitive. People gave me that *stay-at-home mom* look—like I'd wasted my degree on diapers and lunchboxes. Ryder's girlfriend once cackled that I'd been voted Most Likely to Get Married, Stay Home, and Homeschool Eleven Kids.

"Well," Ryder said, his voice shifting, "I'm calling because I volunteered to facilitate care for Jay Hensley's kids—to make sure their needs are met and confirm you want to move forward." It wasn't official authority so much as small-town logistics—there were only so many people to cover bases in a place where everyone was either related or rubbing elbows every day. Great. He was one of the boys who used to run the high school, always angling for control. Another power grab. His tone went flat, all business. "It's pretty cut and dry. We confirm best interests. If not, foster care or another relative. But since you already went to court, it should be straightforward."

Ugh. The word tasted bitter as old coffee.

"How are they doing?"

I wasn't sure how to answer that.

Getting to know the kids after almost three years was like uncapping a bottle of your favorite soda, only to find someone had swapped the sugar for sand.

Don't get me wrong—I'd loved those little buggers. But after Jay moved away, they vanished from my rearview. I did not even know they had returned to town. Whatever happened in the gap, they'd come back quieter—still as the stuffed animals lining Annie's closet.

Shane survived on a steady diet of *I'm sorrys*. Molly sneered like I was the stranger who'd stolen her purse, makeup caked on thick—angry, defiant, mascara smudged beneath her eyes. Daisy...Daisy just cried. And cried. And wouldn't let me touch her.

I ordered pizza. They nibbled and pushed it away. Midnight, I baked chocolate chip cookies. Next morning, I tried again. Peanut butter and jelly. Pizza pockets. Chocolate milk. Every comfort food I could think of.

Nothing landed.

Eventually, each took a pre-packaged ham-and-cheese meal kit—Annie's usual. They sat cross-legged on the floor, pecking at the plastic trays like sparrows on a winter sidewalk.

God, I wished they'd come with directions.

"Any idea where your dad went?" I tried, voice gentle.

Blank stares. Like I'd spoken another language.

Shane's face flushed, mouth pinched, knuckles white around the lunch kit.

"How about ice cream?" I rushed in, already elbow-deep in the freezer, slamming a frosty gallon onto the table. "Or peanut butter cookies, or—" I trailed off, hearing the desperation in my own voice.

And now, admitting it to Ryder—"Well, obviously force-feeding them junk food isn't helping," I said, aiming for lightness. No laughter. That bridge was already ashes.

Ryder started listing agencies, as if I couldn't keep the fridge stocked. I shrank inside—like maybe I wasn't enough. I trusted my training. What I didn't trust was my right to step back into a role I hadn't failed at—but hadn't been allowed to keep.

When he asked to talk to the kids at school the next day, I just agreed.

Later, hunched over my sticky kitchen table, I tried to trace the last time Jay had been seen alive. The kitchen smelled faintly of dish soap and microwaved noodles, sticky with the residue of a long, unproductive day. I wondered if anyone else had filed a missing person report—if anyone besides me would even think to. Probably not.

I dug out the old photo I had of Jay, jotted down a description, and pulled up the last location he'd been tagged on social networks. Then I took it all to the police department and handed the bundle to Susan Little, the civilian clerk at the front desk, palms damp against the plastic sleeve.

She hesitates—not long enough to be obvious, but long enough that the pause slices through the hum of the waiting room. Her eyes dart toward the door, then snap back to the desk. The pen in her hand halts mid-stroke. "This isn't..." she starts, then stops. Clears her throat. "This isn't really my area."

I wait, refusing to fill the silence. Let it stretch, taut as fishing line. She lowers her voice, just a fraction. "If there were more," she says carefully, "or if this were framed differently, someone else might take a look."

"Someone else," I repeat.

She nods once—too quick. "But as it stands—" The pen comes down, firm and final. "—there's nothing I can do." She slides the paperwork toward me, her fingers lingering at the edge, like she's not quite ready to let go. "I'm sorry," she says, and this time it sounds like it costs her something. Then she straightens, moment gone, voice clicking back into place. "If anything changes, you can always follow up."

I could've made noise—asked for a supervisor, insisted on a report—but I knew how that ended. Polite nods. Closed ranks. My name quietly filed under "difficult."

I take the papers. She doesn't look at me again. I stare down at the picture—Jay caught mid-laugh on a dock, sunlight bleaching the edges—one of the last he ever posted.

They stopped cold three and a half months ago. One minute, a selfie with a blonde on a sun-bleached dock; the next—nothing. The thought had been circling all day, and now it snapped into place like a dropped call that never reconnects. As if he'd slipped out of focus, leaving only static where his life should be. The phone rang as I sat back down in my car in the parking lot. I let it ring once. Twice. Something in my chest already knew who it would be.

"Misty," It was Noah Ryder again. I squirmed in my seat knowing the man was somewhere else in that police station— hadn't bothered to get up and face me—so the news he was giving me probably wasn't good. There was no warmth left in his voice. "I just wanted to give you a heads-up before you hear it from someone else."

I closed my eyes.

"School administration reached out this afternoon," he continued. "Concerns were raised. Not accusations. Just... questions."

About routine. Stability. Temporary arrangements.

"They're scheduling meetings," he said. "Tomorrow."

"With who?" I asked.

"With everyone."

I stared at the dark screen of my phone after the call ended, the picture of Jay still on the table, face frozen mid-smile like it belonged to someone else now.

Tomorrow wasn't about finding Jay. The realization came fast, too fast to feel clever. Tomorrow was about whether I was allowed to keep his kids. That was when I realized this wasn't just a custody mess—it was the beginning of something else, and I didn't yet know how bad it could get.

It wouldn't be official yet. Not until the forms caught up. There would be polite emails first. Calendars checked. Boxes ticked in offices I'd never step into. I knew how this worked.

What I didn't know—what no one ever asked on the forms— was whether I could actually do it. Whether wanting to was the same thing as being able. Three more kids wasn't a decision. It was a weight, already settling, already real.

By the time anything landed in my mailbox, the decisions would already be made—dressed up, reasonable, and final. Apparently, I'd be expected to look the same.

Chapter −3

The night after school starts, supper is still quiet.

Silence hangs heavy, thick enough to press against my skin and cling to the buttery warmth of fried chicken. My legs stick to the vinyl seats; the harsh overhead light glares down. Even mismatched chairs from the garage—hard, cold—can't distract from the hush. Shane, tall and lanky, somehow looks small, the folding chair pressing into his ribs until he seems more bewildered four-year-old than teenager. He's six foot already, bookish but sturdy, hinting at an athlete's frame. He keeps shoving his brown hair back with jittery fingers, voice tight with nerves as he thanks me, again and again, for supper.

Supper's nothing special: fried chicken breasts from the freezer, greasy French fries from Tom's Small Town Market, spaghetti noodles slicked with too much margarine—Annie's only food group lately. The kitchen smells of old oil and burnt breading, clinging to my hair and skin. No time for better; my head still buzzes from hours hunched over paperwork at Wally's, my fingers raw from mopping the Pinehaven School District Office. The gas tank's nearly empty. Forty-two bucks in the bank. The fridge holds only day-old hotdogs and some limp bacon. Payday's four days away. Exhaustion settles over me, thick and inescapable.

We sit around the table. Annie stabs at her food, fork clattering against her plate in a rhythm that sets my teeth on edge. She growls at everyone, low and feral, rolling her eyes so hard I worry they'll stick. Shane just stares, bewildered, fingers raking through his hair. Freckles dust his nose—a reminder he's still just a kid. Daisy slumps, elbows on the table, face crumpling as silent tears streak down her cheeks. Molly, thirteen and a half and worn thin by playing grown-up, lips smeared neon-pink, mascara thick as tar, shoots Daisy a glare. "Shut up," she snaps, her voice slicing the air.

"I miss Nacho." Daisy's voice cracks, hiccupping. She stands abruptly, chair crashing to the floor. A wail bursts out— so high-pitched the windowpanes quake. I half expect them to shatter.

"Who is Nacho?" I shout, trying to be heard over the chaos. As soon as I move to stand, the kids look like they might dive under the table. A stuffed animal? Some cheese-obsessed classmate? Before I can ask, Daisy collapses to the floor, her scream raw and animal, vibrating in my chest. Shane leaps up, grabbing her waist, hands trembling. "Stop it, please, Daisy. Stop!" he begs, voice breaking. I catch him whispering, "— she'll make us go. They'll take us to foster care or something." That was when I understood—Shane wasn't guessing. He'd already crossed into the version of the world where his dad didn't come back.

Then Annie goes full feral: jumps onto the table, crawling on all fours, knees scattering plates, palms slapping through French fries, neighing like a wild horse. She rears up, knocks over two glasses of milk. Part of me wonders if something's wrong with her—if I'd touch horns under her strawberry-blonde hair. Maybe I should pick up a Bible next trip to the store. (Not really, but…)

I am halfway between rising and diving down to help Shane who took a fist to the jaw. I catch Molly sobbing into her hands. And there's a knock of knuckles three times at the door.

"Shat." The word slips out—my sanitized curse, after Annie once parroted the real thing to her teacher. Daisy flips something into the air; I feel it hit my head and tumble away. Every head snaps toward me, eyes wide and startled. For a heartbeat, the room holds its breath, tension crackling. Then Annie drops to all fours, rolls across the table, barking and yelping as she slides off the edge. Chaos erupts again—wild, uncontainable—and this time, I let it. There's no fighting the storm.

When I open the door, Ryder stands there, leaning hard on his cane. His posture is careful, guarded—the way it's been since the fire. He isn't eighteen anymore. But his eyes are the same: warm, brown, creased like they're hiding a smile.

The girls used to giggle over him—heart-shaped mouth, that easy, hometown-boy handsomeness. Ryder was always good-looking, pick of the hometown litter, not just for his athleticism but for wearing it all without trying.

Now... maybe not so much.

The smile's gone. Something in his eyes is dulled, whatever once lit them burned out. I'd heard his love affair with his high school sweetheart—the one everyone thought would last—hadn't.

His gaze flits past me, drawn to the noise inside. Next to him stands a hulking woman, making the doorway feel smaller.

She's tall, broad, with brown hair to her shoulders. There's a bone-deep strength to her—less gym, more granite. Shoulders thick under a hoodie, arms corded, hands big enough to palm a basketball. Bleach-blonde hair chopped short and uneven, dark roots creeping in. She's holding a big cardboard box on her hip, like it weighs nothing.

I shift automatically, trying to block the view inside. It doesn't help. Ryder's gaze drops. Then mine does.

A square of processed cheese—somehow—completes its slow fall from my hair, landing between us.

I pretend it didn't happen.

"We brought some food," Ryder says, voice tight, nodding at the box.

The woman barks a laugh, then clamps her mouth shut. "Sorry. That just—yeah."

"This is a bad time," I say.

"No kidding," she says, cheerful but not unkind. Her eyes glance over the chairs, table, floor, edge of the hallway—taking everything in, whether she wants to or not.

Ryder clears his throat. "She's helping with deliveries."

"Community service," the woman adds. "Reckless driving. Three times. Kids don't teleport to school, no matter what the judge thinks."

"He said they wouldn't need to teleport if you got them up earlier, Elle," Ryder says, dry. He glances at me. "We're working on her driving skills. Or trying."

A crash detonates inside the house.

Ryder grips his cane tighter. "That... doesn't sound good."

The woman winces, shifting the box. "Oof. Yeah, that's a rough one."

She looks down—not looming, just present—and gives my arm a quick, friendly punch, like we're old friends. It hurts. I step back. "I don't need charity. But thank you."

Another bang. Annie's barking. Shane shouts Daisy's name. Molly's screaming cuss words I don't think I've even heard before.

I start to close the door. Ryder sticks his foot out, catching it, ready to barge in. Daisy rounds the corner, hands out, looking ready to play Red Rover and crash past me. Shane barrels after her, sliding to a stop in his stocking feet, fingers catching Daisy's collar. I spot a red mark along his cheek where Daisy clipped him at the table.

"Misty, can you give us a moment?" he says. I swallow hard, standing awkward as he nods to Shane. "Son, I'd like to speak with you privately in the other room."

I'd regret it later. Ryder left with a funny pinch in his lips, a shadow of something unsaid. From the kitchen, I caught snatches of his voice—asking each kid if they felt safe here. After Annie's full-on demonic episode at dinner, with me dragging her out as she bucked and neighed, I wouldn't have blamed them for thinking an exorcism was next. I didn't hear their answers. I just moved aside when Ryder left through the front door, nodding once, nothing else. Except I asked him what the police are doing about finding Jay, did they have any clue where he'd gone?

He looks me up and down, his gaze stopping just below my chin, the way someone does when they've already decided how honest they're going to be. "You dated him," he says carefully. "You know him better than anyone here, don't you think?" He hesitates, then adds, "He was always moving around, always dropping the kids with a nanny or a neighbor. He'll probably show up next week acting like he'd never left at all."

I wasn't so sure. Later, out of a morbid curiosity, I asked

Molly what Ryder talked to them about. "He kept asking if we felt safe here." She just shrugged.

"Do you?"

"I don't feel safe anywhere."

Chapter –4

Two nights after the knock, Nacho should've been dead.

Five years old, grossly obese, mean as hell— built like a wrecking ball that swings back. Daisy hid him in her closet with six opened cans of cat food and a pitcher of milk minutes before the police came that night, which tells you everything about how fast things went wrong.

I know this because I had to pry my way into the house with a tire iron from my trunk.

Shane said they didn't hide a key under the mat or in a planter like normal people. Their dad wouldn't let them. Paranoia masquerading as discipline—one of his favorite tricks.

Nacho was already a problem back when I lived there. Wide-mouthed hisses. Murderous paws that latched onto skin and raked hard at the first sign of affection. The kind of animal you respect because it clearly wants you dead.

"I hope to God it's still alive," I mutter as Shane clasps his hands so I can boost myself up and slide through the downstairs window on my belly. "And that I don't get arrested breaking into your house."

"Either way, I'm out," he says. "I'm not telling Daisy her cat's dead. And if the cops show up, you're on your own."

I snort. "Ah. There's the Shane I remember."

And I do. He used to bail every time his dad came home early—after I'd let him stay up watching horror movies— leaving me to take the blame. "Same kid who vanished the second your dad's truck hit the driveway," I say. "Left me standing there like I'd forced you at gunpoint to watch a slasher flick."

The house reeks of stale grease and ketchup. No surprise—Shane admitted they'd been living off three of his dad's credit cards, eating drive-thru for weeks. Molly cooked frozen pot pies and pizza once the cards started maxing out and the minimum payments stopped.

I expected clutter—two teenagers without supervision will do that. What I didn't expect was destruction.

Furniture is tipped. Papers litter the floor, as if a mob ransacked the place. I pause, scanning corners and shadows. A loose sheet skitters across the floor, chased by a chill that seeps under the baseboards.

I immediately hate that—the house feels watched. I reach back and pat the window, peering outside. I don't want Shane following me in—and I definitely don't want him seeing the house like this if he didn't leave it this way.

"Stay here and watch," I whisper. "I'll get the cat."

I hesitate, gripping the emergency flashlight from my car. Every other one in my house is dead or dying.

I cross the living room, stepping over papers, skirting overturned furniture. I'm not halfway up the stairs when a dull thump echoes—too heavy for a settling house.

My heart skips. Nacho digging his way out of the closet, I tell myself. Or an intruder. After seeing the mess downstairs, calling the cops on myself suddenly feels reasonable. *Boom.*

I suck in a breath and ease it out. One step. Another. Sweat beads at my temples, the air thick with the scent of old fries and fear.

Above me, something moves—slow, padded footsteps on carpet. The sound is soft, but every hair on my arms rise.

I crouch on the stair, curling into the shadows. A large shape slides along the wall as one of the motion-activated lights flicks on. I know what comes next: each step lighting in sequence. I'd installed them years ago, when the kids were little—terrified they'd tumble down at night. Because I worry. Because I overthink. Because that's my curse. My heart hammers. They have to see me now.

A huge form lumbers past, lugging a white plastic laundry basket overflowing with papers like he was clearing the place out. Step. Step.

I brace myself. Run or fight. Shane is still outside, probably peering through the window, with no idea someone else is inside. The foot hits the third step. Tina Metzger's self-defense drills kick in: don't grapple—use gravity.

I explode upward. My hands grab fabric. I shove with everything I have, adrenaline spiking so sharp I taste bile.

The body goes down hard—headfirst—slamming the railing, tumbling end over end. The basket flies. Papers burst into the air, fluttering like frantic birds. The crash at the bottom is sickening—a dull, wet thud and the sharp crack of wood.

For one breathless second, everything goes still. My ears ring. Dust floats in the air, catching the stair light like snow.

But I'm not stupid. I barrel down the steps, taking a flying leap on the last three, aiming to stomp the center of the jacket. My hand snags the basket. Not exactly lethal, but it'll do. I slam it again and again at the figure scrambling up—he doesn't even try to hit back. It's a man, bulkier than me, reeking of sweat and panic. He careens down the hallway, through the kitchen and pantry, me in hot pursuit, then bursts out the back door. I stop short, the door slamming in my face. He vanishes into the dark.

Two minutes later, I've locked the door, sent Shane out to the car, and told him not to let anyone in. I think he must've caught me wailing on the guy, because he grabs my keys and lopes out while I watch from the window. He looks rattled— shoulders hunched, eyes wide, jaw set like he's bracing for a storm.

Nacho is yowling from the closet when I release him. I scoop him up at breakneck speed before he can bolt, wrapping him in a sheet snagged off the bed because he keeps wriggling free, claws flashing. On my way out, I gather the scattered papers, shove them back into the basket, and sneak everything out the front door.

"Is there something you two need to tell me?"

I lean against the bathroom doorframe two hours later while the older two brush their teeth over the sink. They share a glance they think I don't catch. I'd gone back for the cat pan and food—at least, that's what they thought. The basket of papers the intruder left now sits hidden in my trunk, waiting for them to fall asleep so I can bring it inside.

"Naw," they both answer. Maybe I haven't been around for a couple years, but I still know their tells. Shane must've heard the commotion when the man fell. I'm sure I yelped, and he ran too fast to the car for it to be nothing. Not once did he mention it on the ride home. He just looked relieved when I stuffed Nacho into Daisy's arms.

"Look me in the eyes," I tell Molly, folding my arms at my waist.

"No, and I'm brushing my teeth." Uh huh. I don't buy it for a second.

"There was someone in your house tonight," I say quietly. Molly freezes at the sink, toothbrush hovering midair, eyes darting toward Shane as if waiting for him to decide what happens next. Shane doesn't stiffen at all. His toothbrush keeps moving, steady and deliberate, and that's what finally gets my attention. The pause feels calculated, like he's weighing consequences instead of telling the truth. "They didn't know I was there—that's the only reason I'm standing here now." I chew my lip. "I'm not trying to scare you. But if there's anything I need to know to keep us safe, you have to tell me. If my life or my kid's is in danger, I'll be a hell of a lot angrier if you keep it secret."

Shane spits, rinses, and wipes his mouth with the back of his hand before finally meeting my eyes. "Do you want us to leave?" His answer isn't scared. It isn't defensive. It's practical, the way someone talks when they already have an exit mapped out.

He's a little angry at me, I can tell, and I understand why. He's been a stand-in dad to Daisy for months now, even tried to take over Annie's bedtime ritual when everything else was falling apart. I told him I could handle it, that he could just be a teenager again, but the resentment still sits there, tight in his shoulders. He works his jaw and narrows his eyes to fine slits, just like his dad used to when he was angry with me.

"Ryder says if we don't fit here, he can help us find someplace else."

Why would Ryder say that? The thought sends a prickle up the back of my neck, sudden and unwelcome. "I did not say that at all," I tell them, meeting both their eyes so there's no room to misread me. "I want you to stay. You're like family to me. It takes time to adjust—but we can't have secrets."

But secrets have a way of surfacing anyway, no matter how carefully everyone pretends they aren't there.

Around three in the morning, I hear Shane talking on the phone.

Low voice. Careful. The kind you use when you don't want walls listening. I stand in the hallway, barefoot on cold tile, counting breaths until my pulse stops racing. When I push his door open, he's already curled on his side, eyes closed, phone dark on the nightstand.

"Shane," I whisper. Nothing. I don't wake him. I don't touch the phone. Back in my room, I lie awake staring at the ceiling, replaying the weight of the man I shoved down the stairs, the way he ran without fighting back, the papers scattering like he didn't care if he lost them. And I think about the basket hidden in my trunk. Waiting.

Chapter −5

Wally, my boss, decided I was hotheaded. How he landed on that, I couldn't tell you—maybe it was the lazy, half-baked myth about redheads. He's got a thing for calling me "Ginger" when he's especially smug, and more than once, he's nudged me to lean into the stereotype—play dumb, flirt, act harmless—if it helps him squeeze information from clients.

He calls it "using my assets."

I call it "humiliating."

None of my red-haired brothers are loose cannons. They're calm. Reserved. Fully capable of functioning in polite society without anyone handing them self-help audio like a corrective device.

Though, to be fair, my mother claims she almost renamed me "Spitfire" because of the legendary tantrums I threw from birth. Maybe Wally didn't invent it out of thin air—just, thin character.

That said, I am always trying to better myself.

Six months in, Wally shoved a cassette across his desk like he'd cracked the case of *What's Wrong with Misty*. The label read: *"Calm Yourself. Discipline Your Anger."* The thing looked ancient—creased, sun-bleached, probably recorded in the Reagan era. I had to buy a cassette adapter for my car just to listen.

"It'll help you focus," he said, using that patient, patronizing tone men reserve for women they've diagnosed as the problem.

Normally, I would've tossed something like that in the

trash. But he insisted it was "scientifically proven." Claimed the longer I used it, the more effective it'd be. As if my personality were a software glitch that just needed regular updates.

Then he slid a second tape across the desk. I looked at him from under my lashes, letting my silence do the talking.

"*Be a Warrior. Be Strong.*' That sounds like the opposite," I said. "Like I'm gearing up for a fight."

He pointed his finger at me like a toy pistol and clicked his tongue. "Bang. I'm just not convinced the first one'll work. You're a wildcard, Ginger—"

"Misty," I cut in, my hands curling into fists despite myself.

He grinned, completely unfazed. "Every time I see you, Misty, you look like you're sitting on a powder keg with a match in your hand—a real live wire. And if that short fuse ever blows, I want you ready to protect yourself."

Ha. Ha.

I do listen to them—a lot. I put up one of the heavy, long punching bags in my garage. It is too small and too filled with junk to fit my car inside. I put some music on my phone and play *Be a Warrior. Be Strong* and punch out my frustrations for about an hour each night after Annie goes to bed.

Now, I also listen to the calming tape with the kids crammed in the car, arguing over who gets dropped off at school first. I keep a copy of each tape on the dash and another on my phone, just in case disaster strikes mid-commute.

According to the label, "*Calm Yourself. Discipline Your Anger.*" promised to reduce stress and help me "harness emotional control." The voice on that tape is low and smooth—a woman who sounds like she moonlights as a jazz singer, confident in a way that feels manufactured.

"I am in control of how I feel," she murmurs this morning as I edge through a snarl of traffic, the air alive with the bitter punch of double espresso in my hand and something sour— maybe the ghost of a forgotten lunchbox—lingering under the seats.

I echo her, trying to match her sultry tone, though my voice cracks somewhere between conviction and too much caffeine.

Shane snickers in the front seat, his sneaker thumping against the console in time with his laugh. "Is this the one you listen to in the garage when you're fighting that old bag?"

"Nope. That one gets me in fight mode." I'm stopped at a red light, hands locked around the wheel hard enough that my knuckles ache. "This one's the opposite. You'd better hope this tape works—or change that attitude," I add. "Or I'll switch back."

I try to smile past it. I don't think I pull it off. I probably look like a rabid dog deciding whether to lunge.

"Ptoom, ptoom, ptoom," Shane says, pitching his voice high and theatrical. He shadowboxes the air with both fists. "I'm Misty and I'm gonna punch your lights out. But only if you're a mouse—"

He stops short, grinning at his own joke, pleased with himself in that way that says he knows exactly where the line is and enjoys leaning over it.

I don't laugh.

The light turns green.

"I choose to feel calm," the voice says.

I repeat it again. Molly sniffs a laugh.

From the backseat, Annie shrieks, "Daisy touched my backpack!" Her voice ricochets through the car, sharp as a fire alarm.

"I choose to feel happy," the voice insists.

"I choose to be happy." I repeat it louder, ignoring them.

There's a scuffle—a sneaker smacks the back of my seat, jolting me forward. The air fills with bubblegum and the cloying, curdled tang of a milkshake spilled long ago without me knowing.

"I am in control of how I feel," she tells me.

I repeat it, then notch the volume higher, as if sheer decibels might drown out the chaos.

"I choose calm."

Another notch.

"I choose happiness."

By the time I pull into the school lot, the tape is bellowing over the sound of my children waging war. Shane's twisted halfway around in the front seat, brandishing a rolled-up homework paper like a sword, while Molly referees and Daisy shrieks in protest.

"I AM IN CONTROL OF HOW I FEEL," the woman announces, sultry and unwavering.

"I AM IN CONTROL OF HOW I FEEL!" I screech back, slamming the car into park hard enough to make the dashboard rattle.

Parents stare. A crossing guard freezes, halfway through a sip of coffee.

"I CHOOSE TO FEEL CALM," the tape declares.

I scream it back, rolling down the window as Shane and Molly bail out, darting onto the sidewalk and vanishing into the stream of backpacks and lunchboxes.

"HAVE A GOOD DAY!" I holler after them, my voice trailing over the tape's relentless affirmations.

They duck their heads and nearly run, disappearing into the crowd.

A few moms clustered at the curb go quiet. One turns. Then another. Their conversation dies as they stare at me in my car, windows down, tape still blaring. I give them my best wild-eyed grin, then throw both hands up, palms wide, like I'm refereeing a brawl only I can see.

I bark over the tape, "What?"

The tape purrs, *"I choose to feel calm."*

"I SAID—YOU GOT A PROBLEM?" I snap, waving my arms like I'm conducting an orchestra of chaos.

The nearest mom flinches. Another clutches her purse closer. They whip their heads away in unison, suddenly absorbed in car doors, purses, shoelaces—anything that doesn't involve making eye contact with the woman screaming affirmations at a cassette player.

I glance back. Daisy and Annie sit frozen in their booster seats—hands folded, eyes huge, lips zipped tight. The silence is sudden, electric.

A tiny, wicked smile curls at my lips.

I reach forward and flip off the tape, the sudden hush ringing in my ears.

I choose silence. For now.

Chapter −6

The laundry basket the intruder dropped at Jay's house was flimsy, white, and unmistakably cheap. It was the brittle kind that always cracks in one corner—the kind you see stacked in the fluorescent-lit aisles of the Pinehaven Discount Dollar Store. That's why I'm planning on hitting the dollar store later, hunting for the origin of a purchase that doesn't fit Jay at all. Jay prefers handwoven rattan baskets flown in from unpronounceable islands. Four hundred dollars a piece, one for every bathroom, each basket as curated as an art installation. Jay replaces his towels every three months— three hundred a set—as if luxury were a subscription. This plastic basket was an alien artifact in his manicured world.

When I plopped the basket on my kitchen table, the cheap plastic gave off a faint whiff of artificial lemon, and the half-peeled blue sticker looked like it was shedding its own skin. But it wasn't the basket that made my breath catch; it was what tumbled out when I upended it. Seven manila folders, battered but neatly stacked, fanned across the old Formica, each tagged with a color copy of a driver's license and a four-page dossier. Someone had gone to impressive lengths to keep these together—and even greater lengths to make sure they ended up right here.

Jay never noticed details. He was the type to toss dirty socks on the floor and expect them to materialize, clean, in his drawer by morning. For years, that was my role: girlfriend, nanny, cook, cleaning crew. Looking back, I wonder which hat I wore most often, and whether "girlfriend" ever really made the list.

Sometimes I suspect I was just the live-in help, because if you'd asked me what Jay did for a living, I couldn't have told you precisely. He told people he was a freelance writer. Maybe a journalist.

I only knew that much because he was always gone, always somewhere else, and when I asked about it, he'd laugh and say, "Don't worry your pretty little head about it." Which— yes—that's condescending. I see that now, clear as fluorescent light on linoleum. But back then, it mattered that he never complained. For a single, working mom, finding a man who gets the daily chaos—who doesn't resent it—feels rare enough to trade away a few questions.

In retrospect, though, I can see it clearly.

Me—his now former girlfriend—must have been at the bottom of his agenda. But maybe I should have been at the top, because aside from the kids, I seem to be the only one concerned he's lying in a ditch somewhere, dying.

I should probably leave this to the police. They laughed at me when I stopped by the station later, with only twenty minutes to spare before I had to pick up the kids from school.

The Pinehaven Police Station is a two-story brick time capsule that smells faintly of old floor wax and stale coffee. I hate going in there. It isn't just the dingy mid-century furniture or the scuffed tile. Walking through those doors feels like stepping into the past, the air heavier, thick with stories and secrets. It was the first place I tried to land a real career, and instead, I crash-landed a thousand miles away, scraping by as a janitor and part-time bookkeeper.

Still, I went in to ask whether they had any leads on Jay.

I hated going back, but the kids deserved to see me try. The kids hadn't asked yet, but I knew they would. If not for myself, then for them, I wanted an answer.

Back at the station—a place I dread—Officer Thomas Smythe, with his unfashionable buzz cut that makes half the department look like boiled hotdogs, lets his gaze wander around the room. A few bored officers glance up from their ancient steel desks, hiding eye rolls behind paperwork. He greets me. "Well, hello, Missy."

"It's Misty," I correct him. "I'm trying to find out what's going on with Jay Hensley's disappearance. Have you been able to find anything? Where he is, or—?"

He cuts me off, trying for stern but landing somewhere south of condescending. He says Jay will turn up eventually, that it's just like him to disappear and leave the kids with a nanny. He gives me a knowing look, as if I should be in on the joke.

In that moment, I feel like the punchline—the one about Jay dumping his kids on me, or about why a guy like him would ever date a woman like me. I was cautious. Nurturing. Useful. Maybe too useful. I imagine the whole town got a good laugh out of it then, and now they keep circling back to the joke, like it's an old, threadbare knock-knock routine.

"Just give it time. He'll be back," Officer Smythe says, nodding like he's talking to a child. "We're working on it, but we've got higher-priority cases than an adult runaway." He gives a short, forced laugh. "Kids too much for you?" They'd taken the report—technically. The paper existed. The effort didn't. Kids were too much for anyone. But I don't say that.

He turns away, already finished with me. I stand there a beat longer, then leave, my shoes squeaking on the linoleum, the air behind me thick with old secrets.

Either they don't give a damn about Jay, or they know something I don't. It feels like everyone is in on the same secret, and no one will say a word.

I thought at first it was just me concerned about Jay's disappearance. Now there's Beth Ann at the dollar store. She watches me when I stop in after school for snacks, eyes tracking me as I zone out under the fluorescent lights—not concern exactly, more curiosity than anything else, invested in the story as if we're characters in a pulp crime magazine, not people with a shared history.

Beth Ann Givens is the undisputed queen of the Pinehaven Discount Dollar Store. I see her more than I see my parents— maybe that says something about my life, or maybe it says something about Beth Ann.

I spend hours in those over-lit aisles, hunting for snacks that won't dissolve into dust, rummaging through the fridge for half-price cheese sticks. Beth Ann is always there, anchored behind the counter like a retail lighthouse, snapping her wintergreen gum and chatting up every customer as if she's known them forever.

Sometimes I wonder if she's a robot, programmed for small talk and exact change. I've never seen her anywhere else—not in the grocery, not at school events, not even at the gas station.

But I know, from years of waiting in line, that she has two kids: Shenandoah, thirteen, and Dallas, fourteen. Both bleach-blond, both with the same wide, relentless smile and the kind of chatter that fills a room. Beth Ann is beautiful—blue eyes, sun-streaked hair, the sort of face that would stop traffic anywhere else. But in this town, beauty only buys you so much before the invisible hierarchy kicks in and nudges you to the sidelines.

If she lived somewhere that prized novelty, she'd be the talk of the town—the kind of woman a rich man would claim like a prize. Here, she works the register, chews her gum, and watches everyone else's lives parade past. But this is Pinehaven, and everyone knows their place—who matters, who married right, who stayed, who didn't.

I've seen her kids in the store too, sometimes crouched behind the counter on days she can't find a sitter, sometimes home from school, noses red and eyes watery. They're both named for the places they were conceived. Beth Ann isn't married; she claims a new boyfriend every week—at least, that's what she tells the regulars while I juggle armfuls of snacks spilling to the floor, listening in.

Tonight I come in with all four kids after school, and they explode through the doors in every direction, like I've just turned them loose in an amusement park—shouts, sneaker squeaks, the faint tang of grape soda on the air.

"Wow, are those all yours?" Beth Ann asks, then pauses, her expression wavering as realization dawns. "Oh." She leans in, voice dropping, eyes following Molly as she sweeps through the candy aisle, already loading her basket with sugar I'll have to confiscate. "Those are the Hensley kids, aren't they?"

Word's out about Jay. I nod slowly, eyes on a rack of batteries so I won't have to say more.

"I didn't know you were a private detective," Beth Ann says slyly, patting the counter with a manicured nail too perfect for a mom with two kids and a job from dusk to dawn seven days a week. I bet one of those boyfriends does her laundry—my own nails are ragged from work and worry.

At her words, my head snaps up. "Where'd you hear that?"

"Well, nobody really. A guy came in here the other day said he was looking for you and said he thought you were following him in his car—he asked for you by name."

Oh, crud. I press a finger to my lips and scan the store. "What did he look like?"

"Fat. Bald. Big shiny truck."

That's half the men in Pinehaven. Most drive new trucks, even as their trailers collapse. My beat-up SUV always makes me feel like the odd one out. I must be staring, because Beth Ann adds, "About five-eight, two-sixty, greasy mustache curled at the corners." She gestures to the height strip by the door, then twirls her hands over her lip to mimic his mustache.

Oh. George Goodson. Serial husband. His third wife—twenty-two, because George is loaded—thinks he's seeing his first wife again. He is. He just keeps outrunning me on the highway before I can snap a picture. But why is he looking for me now? I shove that thought away. Nobody's close enough to hear.

"Kind of hard to sneak around when everyone knows that's what you do, right?" I say. "Can you keep that to yourself?"

She shrugs. "Sure. Maybe you can find my kids' dad so I can get some child support."

"Are you—" I tilt my head. "Extorting me?"

"Maybe."

"I can't. I work for somebody else," I say. "I'm under contract not to compete with my employer by doing what I do for them—unless you want to pay him a hundred dollars an hour." I nibble my lip and glance around the store. "Or you babysit. You babysit?"

What I really want is to slip back to the laundry aisle and see if any baskets here have a label torn the same way. But another thought needles at me—how easy it would be to sneak into the Hensley house again, just to make sure I hadn't missed anything scattered down the stairs. Cat food. Crap. I can't forget to get a cat pan litter and cat food for Nacho.

"Don't you think it's weird?" she asks finally. "That he just vanished, like on those crime shows, and nobody cares?"

My thoughts snap back. "Yeah. One hundred percent."

She blows a bubble of wintergreen gum, pops it with a perfect fingernail, then tucks the sticky bit neatly back into her mouth. "I listen to crime podcasts after I drop the kids at school. There are a million cold cases out there. People just disappear." She shakes her head, eyes shining with the kind of curiosity that makes my skin bristle. "Never thought it would happen here."

She's about to say more when a crash erupts from the back of the store. I know it's my crew before I even turn.

I wander back to find Daisy and Annie tangled on the floor, wrestling over a bag of cotton candy—never mind that there are six more on the shelf, untouched.

"Pecking order."

Beth Ann has never left the register before. It's unsettling—a little like strolling down the same street you've walked a thousand times, nodding at the dog barking behind the fence, only to look up and see it standing three feet away, this time on your side of the fence, silent and alert. Something about the usual order has been broken as I drag the two girls away from each other suddenly caught in the crossfire, and for a split second, you're not sure what's going to happen next. I flinch when I see Beth Ann standing beside me, arms crossed, watching the girls still try to jam knees into bellies and grip the bag like it's a life raft. She works up another bubble, and that's when I notice her ritual: chew, chew, blow, pop, inhale.

"You know," she says, "like chickens figuring out who gets the best place to roost." She nods at the cotton candy. "Or the best sugar rush. They're just sorting out who's top dog."

I glance at her while I'm shoving my way between the two. She shrugs. "Just saying."

For someone I'd just brushed aside like a candy wrapper, I'm suddenly seeing more to Beth Ann than one of the twenty kids dumped off the school bus at Cherry Ridge Trailer Park or the Year 'Round RV Campground. There's an edge to her I hadn't noticed before. "Yeah," she says, nodding once. "I'll babysit for you if you help me find my ex."

I give a noncommittal nod, but the bargain sits uneasily. Her gaze lingers a little too long on Molly and Shane as they rush to break up the fight, sharp and hungry in a way that makes my shoulders tense. I have the uneasy feeling Beth Ann might ask too many questions—and once she starts, I'm not sure she'll know how to stop.

Chapter —7

By the end of that first school week, the dang white basket still lurks beside the couch, half-shoved into the shadows like it's claimed a permanent spot. I'm bone-tired—work, the kids, the endless cycle. I tell myself I'll deal with it later, which is what I always say about things I'd rather ignore. Sometimes, I pretend Jay will just walk in one day and the basket, with all its secrets, will disappear on its own.

One of the folders has slipped half open. Inside, the papers are creased and dog-eared, their corners fuzzy from too many hands. I nudge it back in place without thinking—then freeze, goosebumps running down my arms.

Benjamin Harrison.

Neat block letters spell out the name at the top of the page. The address below is nowhere near here. Nearly a hundred miles away—far enough that it feels wrong, out of place, a ghost that's wandered into my living room. I flip the page once, then again, before catching myself and snapping the folder shut.

The name means nothing to me, but the paperwork does. Estimates. Job notes. The kind of folders contractors haul from site to site, ink faded, margins scribbled with numbers. I wonder why Jay would have this in his house. I suppose he could be working on a story for his research.

I push the basket deeper under the couch with my foot and mutter that I'll let it go. I don't.

Later, when the kids are distracted, and the house is quiet enough for me to hear the refrigerator's hum and the tick of the kitchen clock, I open my laptop and type in the name. I expect a hundred Benjamin Harrisons. I expect useless results, dead ends.

What I don't expect is how fast it pops up—top of the list, in black and white.

Benjamin Harrison. Local contractor. Last seen leaving a job site. Missing, two years. I stare at the screen until my vision blurs, rereading the same short paragraph. My mind circles back to the basket, the folders, the way that house looked—like someone had been sorting through a life, not just cleaning up a mess.

That's the moment I start watching Shane more closely—wondering what he knows that he's not telling me, or anyone.

Shane is all locked doors. I can't figure out how to get in—how to coax out where his dad's gone, or even basic things like what he likes to eat, what makes him laugh, what he'd do if he ever put his phone down. I've got enough brothers to fill a basketball team, but Shane's still an enigma. He keeps trying to play head of household for Molly and Daisy, always leaping in first, always taking on burdens that aren't his to carry.

A week after Shane moves in, he hovers over me while I'm half-watching TV with the girls. Molly is in her usual spot—legs folded, textbooks cracked open on her lap, glasses perched on her nose, highlighter in one hand and remote in the other. She keeps glancing at her phone, probably checking for messages from girls she's trying to impress. Her long brown hair falls in a perfect sheet, and I notice she's wearing lip gloss again, determined to look like she belongs on the cover of some teen magazine. She'd always been like this under the mascara—control as camouflage. Every few

minutes, she murmurs SAT vocab words under her breath—
"inchoate," "obfuscate"—then, catching me watching, she
blushes and feigns interest in the TV. We're passing a dented
aluminum mixing bowl of popcorn—over-salted, buttery, our
fingers so slick the bowl keeps slipping. Nacho is a beached
whale on Daisy's lap, purring so loudly I feel it in my shins.
Molly absently scratches his ears with her pinky, still reading.
We're all bundled under one ancient quilt from Mom's attic,
still carrying the faint scent of mothballs and lavender
detergent, a patchwork of memories stitched into every
square.

Shane doesn't say anything at first. He just hovers, shifting
from foot to foot, nerves practically sparking off him. When
he finally turns to leave, I catch his sleeve.

"What do you need?"

He thrusts a crumpled sheet of paper at me, eyes fixed on
the carpet. "I want to try out for basketball."

Tryouts happened weeks ago, but a kid in class told him to
ask the coach anyway. He did. The coach said no—flat, no
wiggle room. Too late.

"But could you maybe call him and try?" he mumbles, voice
trailing off like he already regrets asking.

I take the paper from his fingers, scoot up on the couch, and
slide the popcorn bowl over Daisy's lap. "You want to play
basketball?" I ask. It comes out odd, even to me.

I don't mean it like that. It just slips out, awkward and
uncertain.

"Nah. I don't have to—I just never got to before, you know?
Dad wouldn't take me to practice. You used to. I thought you

Shay Lawless

liked it. Maybe. Never mind. I'm probably not even good."

"You were good when you played rec league."

"Yeah, but I was twelve."

"You don't just stop being good," I say. "You get rusty. You practice."

"I don't even have a hoop." He flings his hands up. "Or even a ball."

He storms out, slams his door, then cranks the TV so loud the walls shudder. He ignores my knock—even when I bang harder, frustration sharp in my fist. I'm not one to cross that line, so I stay put, clutching his paper. Molly finally looks up from her homework and gives me a sidelong glance—half sympathy, half annoyance—then swipes at her mascara with the back of her hand. Daisy just sinks deeper into the couch.

Molly lifts her chin and fixes me with a determined glare. "If he gets to play basketball," she announces, her eyes shining with resolve, "then I want to play trumpet and join the school band."

"Trumpet," I murmur, my voice cracking like a teen dragging its feet toward puberty. I glance at Molly, hoping she doesn't notice my hesitation as she wraps a curl of her hair around her finger. Just what I need—the blaring sound of a band thrumming in my ears. Maybe I can gift the neighbors earplugs for Christmas. Still, I nod. "Sure." I silently pray they still offer payment plans for band instruments—unless inflation has turned a trumpet into a second mortgage.

That's when I spot the name at the bottom of Shane's form.

"Crud." Coach Bradley. Ricky Bradley—the school's favorite bully. He and his entourage of friends—Noah Ryder,

46

Kyle Evans, and Billy Ramsey—ran our school the way a nightclub owner runs a bar: deciding who gets in, who gets humiliated at the door, and wildly overestimating their importance in keeping civilization upright.

Ricky had a thing for me, and not the good kind. My older brother and Ricky played football together—always squabbling over team captain, their rivalry bleeding into everything else whether it fit or not. Ricky's dad was the basketball coach, the local judge—authority stacked on authority in a town this size.

Ricky couldn't make a basket to save his life, but in small towns, guys like him—and guys like his dad—don't need talent, just a title. My own run-ins with him? None of them good. Some of them my fault. He got under my skin, and I pushed back.

Something his buddy Noah Ryder—now county liaison—used to taunt me about—warning I was always poking the bear, tapping me on the nose when he said it. It made everybody laugh. Ricky most of all, which was quite mortifying.

Noah once tried to justify the whole humiliation by saying it kept Ricky from murdering me. In retrospect, it probably did—by giving Ricky back his power. Needless to say, I called Noah Ryder his hitman.

Still, I fill out the form and slide it under Shane's door.

The next morning, I dig out my old spandex shorts, a faded T-shirt, and the closest thing I own to running shoes. It's barely fifty degrees out, but I jog along the sidewalk anyway, timing it just right. Around Fourth and Walnut, I stop to tie my shoe as Ricky lumbers past, sweat already darkening his shirt, extra pounds jiggling with every step.

"Hey, dude! Haven't seen you since—?" I call out, waving like we're old friends.

He stops. I wasn't sure he would. His face is beet red, sweat pouring off him in spite of the chill. He gives me a slow once-over, pretending he doesn't recognize me, though I know he does. He always used that same face as a power grab.

"You sat behind me in English," I say, watching for the glimmer of recognition. I don't add that he used to copy off me. One time, I wrote all the wrong answers on my paper just to watch him fail.

"You're Ray Bailey's little sister."

Ugh. "That I am."

"You look just like him."

"Kind of," I say. "But I'm a girl."

He blinks, like he's just realized it.

"Nice weather to run in," I say, lying through my teeth. "I usually run at night, but figured I'd switch it up. Hey—you coach basketball, right?"

Somewhere in there, things go sideways. I'm still not sure how I end up agreeing to run with Ricky again the next morning—and probably every morning after that. He's off first period, and between dropping the kids off and cleaning admin buildings, I technically have an hour.

A carload of high schoolers cruises by, windows down, whistling and catcalling us in our running gear—making jabs at their school coach talking to a woman, I suppose.

Ricky looks embarrassed.

I take the opening. I mention I'm taking care of Jay Hensley's kids, and I slip Shane's tryout into the conversation like it's an afterthought.

That, weirdly, seals the deal.

It works. Shane gets a tryout. I'm surprised Ricky even considers it. Small-town rules bend for small-town reasons. Tryouts were weeks ago.

Ricky squints, thinking. "That Hensley kid," he says. "Tall. Brown hair. Just started school?"

I nod.

He exhales through his nose, like the decision's already made. Mercy might've crossed his mind. But height sealed it.

Downside: now I'm actually stuck running. Which I hate. And to anyone who knows our past, it looks like I've surrendered—waving a white flag and joining his fan club, just like all the freshman girls did in high school.

Ricky says Shane better know how to shoot, so I start searching online for a used basketball hoop and find one for a couple hundred dollars. Then I head to my parents' house.

Mom still swears she doesn't color her hair, though not a gray in sight. She wears spandex sweatpants, convinced they make her look athletic (she's never exercised a day in her life). Dad is textbook dad—thick red hair, polo shirts, khakis, tennis shoes.

They're both retired, and after a thorough lecture about how I'm in over my head caring for four kids, Mom says, "Misty Dawn, I think it's noble of you to offer those kids a place, sweetie, but they aren't yours. Don't they have family?"

"No, Mom," I say. "They've got nobody."

My mom's a chatterer, a matchmaker, and a full-time recruiter for my future husband. She treats my name like it's a lure she can dangle in front of any available man with a pulse like she believes my hottest selling point and best chance of snagging a mate is my ephemeral name.

Misty Dawn, she'll say, like she's selling a product. Like if she says it enough times at choir practice or a club luncheon, some nice, employed widower will wander over and ask what I'm doing Saturday. I'm pretty sure half her friends don't even know I clean the admin office. In their heads I'm "between jobs" or "figuring things out while I'm looking for a husband," because Mom doesn't brag about her daughter scrubbing toilets any more than she brags about our bank account.

But then again, she also whispers behind a cupped palm to her friends that the only thing I want in a man is that he's loaded. All because I once joked—pure sarcasm—that I find it attractive when men work out and are ripped.

She decided "ripped" sounded too sultry, like I'm some black widow on the prowl, and, to make things worse, she thought it meant rich. So, she switched it to "loaded."

Now, in her friends' eyes, I'm just a shallow girl hunting for some old guy to marry, hoping he'll drop dead and leave me a windfall.

It hasn't happened yet. Hence, without hesitation and probably feeling sorry for their lonely, single daughter they loan me two hundred bucks. Dad says he'll borrow a truck. My brothers agree to sneak the hoop into the backyard as a surprise while I take the kids out for ice cream.

"Are you still working at the school as a janitor?" Mom asks, wrinkling her nose at the word. "There's a teaching job opening at the middle school. You'd be wonderful."

She's always thought I wasted four years of college. She wanted me to be a teacher. I didn't—it bored me. She doesn't know about Wally.

"I think I want to start my own business," I say, watching their eyebrows shoot up.

I don't. But I love watching them side-eye each other, communicating a whole marriage's worth of worry in one glance.

After I leave, I know they'll talk about me—how promising I was, graduating with honors, fourth in my class. Where did they go wrong? All my brothers are teachers, just like them. I'm the odd chick who perched on the edge of the nest too long, and when I finally got nudged, I fell straight to the ground.

Later that night, as I'm brushing my teeth, Molly appears in the doorway, clutching her phone. "If I ever start posting makeup tutorials, will you promise not to laugh?" she asks, her voice small. I tell her I won't laugh, but of course I will—because that's just what you do for the people you're stuck with and lucky to have. I crossed my eyes. And she rolls hers in return, mutters "obfuscate," and disappears down the hall, her brown hair swinging behind her like a curtain.

I tuck the basketball under my bed, the Christmas paper crackling softly as I push it back with my foot. It looks ridiculous there—festive and hopeful in a room that feels anything but. I tell myself I'll give it to Shane in a day or two, once the hoop's in place and he's had time to cool off.

When I straighten up, my eyes land on the living room again.

The white basket hasn't moved.

It's still half-hidden beside the couch, folders slumped inside it like they're waiting. I think about Benjamin Harrison—how he walked off a job site and never came home. I think about Jay, gone without a word. I think about Shane, locking himself in a room and asking for a basketball instead of answers.

Whatever happened to that contractor didn't start with his disappearance.

It started earlier. Quietly. With paperwork that no one bothered to throw away and someone was trying to steal.

And I have the sinking feeling that by the time I figure out how all of this fits together, it won't just be about where Jay went—but why he made sure the kids ended up with me before everything fell apart.

Chapter –8

The John Winslow Recreation Area, aka Winslow Park, sprawls an hour and fifteen minutes from my town—five hundred acres stitched together by fields, scrub, and shadow.

Mom used to say it had promise. Close enough to the beaches to pull visitors inland, far enough to feel like small-town discovery. The kind of place that should've filled local hotels and breathed life into the quieter corners of the county.

Standing here now, it's hard to see what she ever meant.

Unused soccer fields sit in uneven rows, their grass thin and patchy, goal nets sagging like tired mouths. Fences lean at odd angles, zip-tied in places where repairs were promised but never came. A dog park and ball diamond linger nearby, vacant more often than not, their signage sun-bleached and curling at the corners.

A bike path loops the perimeter, its asphalt already cracked by roots. Hiking trails slip into the trees and vanish—sometimes marked only by muddy prints or the glimpse of a squirrel's tail. On weekends, a few kids kick balls across the worst of the fields. Beer cans collect near the dugouts. Fast-food wrappers snag in the weeds. Trash drifts against the fence line where no one's bothered to clean it up in a while.

Even then, the place feels half-awake—like it's remembering what it was supposed to be.

Beyond the edges, the park stops pretending. The grass sinks into marsh. Pines crowd close. Light thins. Sound dulls. The forest breathes damp and resinous, reclaiming what was cleared.

And that's when the names surface again.

The money came. Everyone agrees on that. Grants, development funds, tourism incentives—funneled through the local tourism agency with plenty of paperwork to prove it. Naomi Reynolds and Tyler Maxwell were brought in to manage the visitor bureau, their names popping up in press releases and ribbon-cutting photos, always smiling, always talking about growth.

They were paid well. Better than most people around here.

Naomi Reynolds was young, eager, and fresh out of college—hired on the strength of enthusiasm and a last name the board already trusted. Her father sat on the county commission. Around here, that counted as experience. And gave her the nickname whispered behind palms, Nepo Naomi.

Tyler Maxwell came later—or maybe he'd always been there. Retired, well compensated, and somehow seated on three other tourism and development boards across the county, he spoke fluent grant language and never once mentioned the fields themselves.

Their names are ingrained in my head. Mom brings them up every single time we're forced into a family picnic here— out of spite, because she'd once wanted to open a cozy bed-and-breakfast nearby. She talks about *what could've been* like it's a personal grievance.

Which maybe it is.

Because standing here, with fences sagging and fields forgotten, it's hard not to wonder where all of it went.

On Tuesday nights in the fall, around dusk, the place empties out completely. No cars. No voices. No movement.

Like a place waiting for something.

And none of those places matter to Kylie Winters—except the parking lot, lit harsh and lonely by a single buzzing lamp.

That's where Wally says she meets a man. Always the same routine, the same hush of secrecy thick as used engine oil.

Same day. Same hour. Six o'clock sharp. Twenty minutes, maybe thirty, right after she leaves work, before she goes back to the apartment she shares with her fiancé. At least, that's Wally's story. He's been parked here three weeks, watching, waiting, eating drive-thru fries and jotting in his spiral notebook. Last week, he swore the man in the battered blue junker spotted him and peeled out, gravel pinging off the bumper. If Wally comes back and he sees him again, these two lovebirds will move on to somewhere else, and the game will start all over again, trying to catch them mid-tryst.

Which is why I'm here tonight at 5:30, three lots over, lacing up for a fake run on Wally's usual trail. I'm sore from my run this morning and the day before with Ricky. He's not fast, but he runs for a good hour without stopping. I'm trying not to look like I lied and wasn't a runner. So, I had to keep up. We both hardly talked as we were mostly out of breath. But I did get a tryout with Shane in three days, after school at 4:30 p.m.

Now, I keep pepper spray on my belt—a precaution I hardly think about during early mornings on Main Street with Ricky, unlike those times in the isolated woods or empty lots.

Taser in my pocket. I pat one, then the other—habit, not comfort.

Sweat beads under my collarbone, and the air smells of

pine needles and old sweat socks forgotten in the trunk.

"So are you all good while I run?" I ask, trying for casual. "Twenty minutes, tops."

I catch Molly's eyes in the rearview. She's wedged between two car seats, knees up, textbook splayed open, hair pulled back. I point through the windshield. "There's the trail. You'll see me the whole time."

"Do we have to?" she groans, flipping a page with exaggerated drama. "I've got trig, which is basically suffering. And you still need to talk to the band director and set up a payment plan for a trumpet. They don't loan them out. It's not sanitary—apparently spit valves are a biohazard. I have to sit in the band room without an instrument while everyone else plays. I look stupid."

"Even more reason for me to stay in shape and run tonight," I say, giving my ankles a theatrical flex. "I'm going to have to get another job or mortgage the house to pay for it—or maybe auction off a kidney somewhere online."

That's the official line—what I tell them, what I tell myself. The truth is, I just need a reason to be out here tonight.

What I definitely don't tell Molly is that I already called the school, gutted my checking account with a hefty down payment, and set up a rent-to-own plan for the thousand-dollar trumpet I was expertly upsold—the classic parent trap for those who want their kids to excel, maybe even play in some future college symphonic orchestra. "Because it would grow with her," the salesman said, which apparently means it grows directly into my wallet. Her brand-new trumpet will be waiting for her tomorrow. Let her sweat a little—guardian privilege, even if she's not technically my birth child.

Shane doesn't look up from his phone. "Remember I know better? You used to do this all the time." He mimics me: "'Oh, Shane, let's get ice cream and stake out a guy getting run over by his wife!'"

"That was a one-off," I shoot back. "He barely got a concussion. And I shoved your head down before you saw anything."

"Dad went ballistic when your car was in the background of the newspaper photo."

"So, you know the drill," I mutter. "Lock the doors. Text me if anything feels off."

"—Surveillance," Shane says flatly. "Just call it what it is. You're going to get us shot."

I roll my eyes. "I am not reckless. This is a harmless, quick pic."

"Yeah. I know you."

A car noses in beside us, close enough to fog our windows with exhaust. My stomach tightens. I pretend not to notice, but my knuckles go white on the steering wheel.

Knock. Knock. Knock. The sound's too bright, shattering the hush. All three of us turn to the steamed window. I jolt, heart skipping, as a figure blurs pink in the glass.

Beth Ann.

She's standing there in a cropped pink fleece, neon and out of place, grinning like she's caught a secret.

I'm out of the car in a flash, grabbing her sleeve and hauling her away from the window. "What are you doing here?" I hiss, glancing back at the kids peering out of the windows.

"I wanted to see what you were up to."

"I'm going for a run," I lie, adjusting my ponytail. "Did you follow me?"

"Well… kind of. I was behind you at the light by Tom's Market and you turned toward Winslow." She tilts her head, earrings swinging. "You're doing a stakeout, right?"

"No." I press my hands out. "We are not playing cops and robbers. It's boring, Beth Ann. You can't just tag along."

Over her shoulder, Kylie's little red compact glides into the lot, her movements careful as if she's coasting across thin ice.

"And I need to get across the soccer field right now," I say. "Please, just get back in your car." My voice is sharper than I mean.

"I'll run with you," Beth Ann says, bouncing on her toes. She stops just long enough to chew, chew, blow, pop—her bubblegum snapping like a firecracker—then inhales the sharp scent of wintergreen. "Please?"

I look her up and down—short skirt, fake leather boots that would lose a fight with mud, and a grin that's pure mischief. "You're not dressed for it."

That's when I spot the blue car. Missing bumper, headlights flickering like nervous eyes.

It pauses, engine ticking. Kylie steps out, stretching like this is any ordinary evening. Wally never mentioned jogging—so either she'd changed the routine, or he'd missed more than he admitted. My gaze darts—far side of the lot, a man gets out, mirroring her timing. Something in my gut knots.

"I've got to go," I mutter. "Please. Just get back in your car, Beth Ann."

I start off at a brisk walk—the kind that tries too hard to look casual. Beth Ann's boots click after me, silent and determined as a cat stalking a bird.

Fine. If she follows, that's on her. I don't have time to babysit the dollar store clerk who thinks this is an adventure.

"Speed walk," I mutter. "Mall-walker rules. No talking, no falling behind."

She beams, practically vibrating, like this is the most exciting Tuesday night she's ever had. I just want her to go home.

We cut behind the ballfields, shoulder to shoulder, through brambly undergrowth that tugs at my leggings. The lot disappears behind us. Two minutes pass—my breath clouds in the cooling air. I spot Kylie again in the fading light, jogging alone, pausing to tug at her shoe. A crow cackles overhead.

"So how does this work?" Beth Ann asks, her voice bright and eager. She lifts her fists, throws a couple of pretend punches, then kicks one leg in a clumsy karate move that nearly topples her into a bush. "Am I, like, backup? Or just supposed to collect evidence while you do your thing?" She whips out her phone, faking a couple of shots.

Oh. My. Gosh. I groan inwardly. Of all people to tag along, it's the cashier from the dollar store who barely knows my name—though she's probably done everything short of a background check on her phone during slow shifts.

"We are not playing cops and robbers. I'm not a cop," I mumble. "I'm just getting a short video. And as far as I'm concerned, you're not here at all. You're basically stalking me. So just pretend we're going for a speed walk—and seriously, don't mention this to anyone."

Then, the air sharpens. Something shifts—like the world just held its breath.

When I was thirteen, I learned what it looks like when an ordinary moment turns wrong—how quickly calm tilts toward chaos.

I was walking home late, shortcutting behind the dugout— the only patch of real dark for blocks. A storm was coming, thunder muttering in the distance. My mother made me wear this white poncho that rustled like a trash bag. I hated it. I wasn't even supposed to be eating a popsicle, and I was more worried about the orange syrup dripping down my arm and staining the poncho—giving me away—than I was about the sky breaking open. Until I saw Ricky Bradley, the kind of high school bully who never needed an introduction, and his friends, fists flying, pinning some poor kid beneath a spindly sycamore.

They hadn't seen me. I could have run—my sneakers were already squeaking in the wet grass. But the pitching machine beside the dugout was already plugged in, humming softly, like it was waiting for its next pitch. The air smelled sharp, like cut grass and the electric tang of rain. Because I knew how it would end.

Ricky Bradley's father was a judge.

Even then—before law degrees and titles meant anything concrete to me—I understood exactly what that bought you in Pinehaven. It meant the principal would look the other way. It meant the report would get "misplaced." It meant the boy on the ground would be told not to make trouble. And if I showed up, I'd land squarely on Ricky's personal *Most Wanted* list—marked for the rest of my life.

Ricky would walk back into class the next day with split knuckles and a smirk, and nothing else would happen.

And it didn't.

I glanced to my left and saw the pitching machine parked beside the dugout. I didn't know then what kind of pitching machine it was, only that it was already plugged in and humming softly, like someone had planned to come back for it. I didn't think. I just loaded a ball and fired. I found out the next day it was a professional machine that had been donated, capable of throwing balls at close to a hundred miles an hour.

First pitch: a sharp crack, echoing off aluminum. Next, a grounder that skipped at their ankles. By the third, they broke—screaming, scattering, one tripping in the mud. Wind whipped up, battering my poncho over my head, my hair wild and snapping against my cheeks.

One of them screamed—high, panicked, ghost stories in the making.

By the next day, the story had spread through the school cafeteria like spilled soda—fast, sticky, impossible to clean up. People said the diamond was haunted, and for years after that, nobody went anywhere near it after dark.

Standing in the woods now, watching Kylie, that old cold clarity settles in my chest. I'm thirteen again, heartbeat in my ears, the world narrowed to one sharp decision.

I didn't stand there that night and suddenly learn how the world worked. Growing up and being the youngest and the only girl among five brothers teaches you early that running only makes things worse, because bullies are predators, and once they sense weakness, they like the chase. They follow just waiting for you to tire. They circle. They wait for the easy moment and pounce. I already knew that. All I did was use it.

Then—the man bursts from the brush, barreling into Kylie headfirst. She blinks, startled, and screams—a raw, animal sound. He grabs her by the neck, dragging her backward, fists flying as she thrashes. Her headphones whip loose, bouncing against her shoulder.

"This isn't a lover," I think aloud. "This is a stalker." My pulse hammers. The world narrows to the thud of boots on dirt.

"Call nine-one-one!" I hiss to Beth Ann, whipping around to face her. "Now. Get to the car. Stay with my kids."

And with nothing but adrenaline and momentum, I sprint—pelting through brush, lungs burning, fingers of one hand curling around my pepper spray and my other hand digging out the taser.

Chapter –9

I've never used a taser before. I'm stunned by how fast it drops a chubby, out-of-shape man to his knees—face-down, nearly crushing me. And just as stunned by how quickly he starts to twitch and push up, wild-eyed, once the current ends. Still, it's enough. Enough for those two little prongs sunk at the base of his neck to do their work. Enough for Kylie Winters to wrench herself free and stumble away.

Everything comes in flashes—broken pieces, half-thoughts, fragments of training surfacing too late. Once a man is down and the taser stops, it's only seconds before adrenaline floods him and he can explode back to his feet. There isn't much else I can do. Tina always said the heel was faster than the foot.

I drive the heel of my boot into his side, scrabbling for the pepper spray, and unleash the stream straight into his face.

Mental note—filed way too late to be useful: never spray into the wind.

I get it too—a mouthful of fire that scorches my tongue, stings my eyes shut. I'm choking when he comes up swinging, and suddenly everything is ugly and loud—me gasping, kicking, screaming, flailing. I'm running on noise, panic, and whatever animal instinct still sparks inside me.

My fist slams into his jaw, knuckles buzzing from the impact. If he'd been bigger, it might not have mattered, but I catch him clean on the chin and he reels sideways. My knee jerks up on its own, smashing into his crotch so hard my toes curl in my shoes. He lets out a guttural, animal sound I'll never forget.

Then—shouting behind me. A man's voice, then a woman's. For a split second, I know exactly what's running through his mind.

Backup.

He panics. Drops, stumbles up, and bolts for the parking lot, shoes slapping wild on asphalt.

Swiping at my burning eyes, I know I should stop. Any one of my brothers would've known better. I don't. Panic and survival flip a switch, and I'm sprinting after him before my brain can catch up. The closer I get, the more certain I am he'll whirl and blast me with whatever's left in him.

Just as he slows, a shadow vaults the soccer-field fence— smooth, fast, almost graceful. Hands clamp the top rail. Ten pounding steps. Then—a full-bodied tackle drives him into the grass, hard enough to knock the wind from both their lungs.

I barely stop myself from plowing into them—skid sideways, stumble, heart hammering in my throat.

The woman on top of him is all muscle and intent—a full-grown lion pinning a wounded warthog. He's still bucking, still swearing, still half-alive beneath her. I wince.

Please let the kids not hear any of this—the snarling, the scraping, the sound of bodies tearing up grass.

Her name clicks into place.

Elle. What is she doing here?

Then the balance of power shifts.

As mighty as Elle is, she's no match for a gun.

I see it the same second she does—the flash of black as he claws something free from his pocket, compact and ugly, fitting his fist too well to be anything else.

"Elle!" I lunge forward and shove her hard. "He's got a gun!"

She rolls instinctively, clean and fast. The man scrambles, comes up on one knee, then his feet, bolting straight for the tree line. Branches whip back as he crashes through the brush, gone before I can even think about chasing him.

Twenty-two minutes later, the park is crawling with uniforms.

Flashlights cut through the undergrowth. Radios crackle. Someone tapes off the path like it might still matter. They work it like a real scene—photographing the grass where he went down, flagging footprints near the fence line, sweeping for dropped evidence. They fan out, methodical, calling his description into the dark, but it's already too late. He's had a head start, and he knew exactly where he was going.

The car was stolen. The plates don't match the vehicle. The VIN comes back clean—clean enough to be useless. Whoever he was, he didn't belong to the car any more than he belonged here.

While Shane very helpfully throws me under the bus with the police, I find out he'd been texting Ryder the entire time—before we even reached the park, and after. Ryder and Elle had been out on one of their competitive, road-rage driving rallies when the messages came through. They'd made a wild U-turn and gunned it straight for us.

I had no idea Children's Services would be waiting when we got home. The house looked normal from the outside—lamp glowing in the living room window, porch steps scattered with shoes.

Ryder did.

He tells me, right there in the parking lot, that maybe it'd be better if the kids were placed somewhere else for now—until I take some classes, or they find someone with more experience. The words are a punch to the sternum. The kids had just started to open up. Daisy, who'd been sleeping in Annie's room, padded in last night and curled up beside her while I read. Molly asked if she could go back to the house, clean out her closet, bring the rest of her clothes home. I said yes. I was going to help her pick what to keep.

Maybe Shane is jealous, I tell myself as we drive. He's quiet in the back seat, chin up, almost proud—like this was the outcome he'd aimed for all along.

As I pull into the driveway, a county car glides in behind me—headlights sweeping the yard.

Rita Farnsworth. Children's Services. Her shoes crunch on the gravel as she steps out, clipboard hugged to her chest.

Mom and Dad are already outside. So are my brothers, Billy and James, huddled by the porch like they're bracing for a storm. The basketball hoop stands in the yard, freshly set, a big red bow tied to it. The Christmas-paper-wrapped basketball squats underneath, bright and ridiculous against the damp, green grass.

Rita steps forward and hands the kids three black garbage bags—cheap plastic rustling, handles stretching in their small fists.

"Go get your things," she says gently, her voice padded with sympathy that doesn't quite reach her eyes.

"Maybe it's for the best, honey. They were a handful," my

mom says, voice sugar-sweet and sharp. "You've got your whole life ahead of you. You don't need three half-grown kids running your life. Go back to school or teach—"

"Shut up, Mom," I snap.

Ryder stands awkwardly, eyes fixed on anything but the basketball hoop and the lonely ball beneath it. Shane saw it too—his face dropped, chest caving in, before he took his garbage bag and disappeared inside. I just stood there in the dark, the window's gold light splashed onto the drive, Annie's hand in mine as she whispered, "Where are they going? Are they going to be alright?" I felt her tears soaking my knuckles. Daisy blinked up at the stranger who led her inside to fill her bag, not understanding any of it.

Jaw grinding, I stomp over, scoop up the basketball, and thrust it into Ryder's hands. "He's got a tryout Thursday at four-thirty. Make sure he gets there." I fix him with my best 'don't test me' glare. "And Molly's trumpet is coming in tomorrow at school. Make sure she puts her name on it—first and last—so big even the janitor on the other side of the building can read it so it doesn't get stolen." I lean in, lowering my voice like I'm confessing a secret. "I couldn't spring for the extra ten bucks a month for the insurance plan."

And just like that, the house empties—all but me and Annie, and the echo of everyone else.

I step onto the porch and catch Edna Jefferson across the street, peering out her window at me and Annie standing there alone. She doesn't even pretend not to be watching this time.

She shakes her head slowly, like she's already decided something, then drops the curtain and disappears.

Chapter −10

I don't sleep. I lie on my back, counting the shadows on the ceiling, replaying everything until it blurs. Every choice feels wrong. Every step forward is another trapdoor. Sometimes I wonder if failure is the only thing I'm truly good at. Even two hours of boxing the bag to the screech of the affirmation tapes aren't working.

A draft of cold air snakes under the window, carrying the sharp tang of rain and last night's burnt toast. Daisy and Annie had snuck into the kitchen and jammed six slices of bread into the toaster, giggling like conspirators, and they would have set the house on fire if I hadn't followed the sound and yanked the plug in time.

My shirt sticks to my skin with sweat I can't shake. Wally calls the next morning. He skips small talk. Doesn't ask if I'm okay or what happened. Just launches into yelling—about the client, the money, how this makes *him* look. I let him rant because arguing feels pointless. On some level, I've already decided this is my fault, even though I know better.

Apparently Kylie's fiancé didn't take it well when she found out he'd hired someone to follow her. She broke it off. He refused to pay. Case closed, at least for him.

Just like that. One crisis collapsed into paperwork and silence.

No one mentions that she might be dead if I hadn't been there. No one brings up the taser, or the way she shook afterward, or how she kept whispering "thank you" like it might be revoked. None of that factors into the math.

All they see is a mess. Bloodless, inconvenient, expensive. All they bill for is inconvenience. Not the bruises, not the fear, not the way I triple-check the locks before I sleep. And somehow, I'm the one left holding it.

The kitchen clock ticks—a little too loud, too fast, like it's keeping score. The phone rings again before I've even made coffee, the sound sharp and impatient—like it's annoyed I didn't learn anything overnight.

"I looked at your report," Wally says the second I answer. Papers shuffle in the background—his signature move, even when he's nowhere near his desk. "Your timestamps are sloppy."

"I was pepper-sprayed," I say, staring at the cheap laminate countertop, one hand pressed to my temple where it still stings. "He had a gun."

"That explains the spelling," he snaps. "Not the gaps."

That's Wally's version of mercy. He doesn't comfort. He corrects. People don't interest him, but loose ends do. Files that don't close gnaw at him—it's the closest thing he has to a conscience.

"She would've been hurt," I say quietly. "You know that."

"And what about that woman who jumped in to help? What if she'd gotten shot?" Wally's breath hitches, just a fraction, like he's about to say something human and thinks better of it. "The point is he's not paying. He hired us to watch, not play hero."

The word "hero" comes out like something sticky he wants scraped off his shoe.

My jaw aches. I want to argue, but the words stick. I

swallow. "Did nobody think I saved her life?" Did he really not realize this whole mess started with him—because he mistook stalking for a clandestine affair?

There's a pause—not warm, not human. Just the faint hesitation of someone annoyed by a truth he doesn't want to account for. A delivery truck rattles past outside, shaking the window glass.

I count three beats before Wally answers. "This isn't a morality contest, Misty," he says. "It's a business. You want credit for saving lives, join the police department."

"I tried that," I mutter. No one laughed then, either.

He always moves too fast, like he's afraid boredom might catch him. He barrels on. "You escalated. You chased. You made it messy. He's threatening legal action. I'm the one who gets to deal with that. And now we've got police asking questions. We have a man on the loose who was stalking a woman."

"*I almost got killed—*" *Because you were wrong about Kylie Winters*. I stop before I get fired, heat rising in my voice.

Wally knows what I was going to say. Silence, thick enough to hear the street outside, footsteps echoing on wet pavement. Then his voice hardens, brittle as glass.

He exhales, then says, "Everybody only gets so many screw-ups. This was one of yours. You just used one up."

The call ended there. Wally likes clean breaks, no lingering. He hates messes he can't sweep away.

I stare at the phone long after the screen goes dark. My reflection floats ghostlike in the glass—haunted, unmoored.

My tongue feels thick, my mouth dry as old wool. The

phone rings again, a number I don't recognize this time. I almost let it go to voicemail. I'm done explaining myself for the day. But something about the timing needles at me, and I answer.

"Hello?"

"Misty?" The voice is female, hesitant, like she's already bracing for me to hang up. "It's Beth Ann."

I sit up straighter. "How did you get my number?"

There's an embarrassed little laugh on the other end. "That woman—Elle," she says. "She comes into the dollar store all the time. Like you do."

I wait.

"We're kind of in the same bracket," Beth Ann goes on, rushing now. "Broke moms. You know, women with kids who don't go out and get high or anything. We get our little hit buying stuff. Not real shopping—just...a candy bar, or a clearance candle, or something we don't need but makes the day feel less heavy for five minutes."

I can picture it perfectly.

"The dollar store's where we all end up," she says. "Elle's got two boys. The ones with kids and bills and not enough time or money to be the women who shop up on Main Street and live in those big houses. It's cheaper than therapy."

She pretty much summed it up.

"I just wanted to check on you," she says, her words spilling out faster now that she's started. "After...everything. Elle was pretty shaken at the park. That guy pulled a gun on you two. You could have—" She stops short of saying it, but the word hangs between them. "It's weird. I keep thinking about it, and it felt wrong not to call." She hesitates, then adds, her tone shifting, "You were seriously badass with those kicks, by the way."

I can hear her grunting on the other end of the line, picture her acting it out—punching the air, throwing clumsy karate kicks at no one in particular.

"Weird how?" I ask.

Another pause. "Like I stuck my nose somewhere it didn't belong," she admits. "I didn't know what you were doing. Or who you were following. I swear, I didn't. I just thought—" She exhales hard. "I thought it looked interesting. Like something to break the routine."

Adventure, she doesn't say, but it hangs there anyway, bright and dangerous as a live wire.

"I had no idea it would turn into... that," she adds quietly. "I keep replaying it and wondering if I distracted you, or got in the way, or made things worse just by being there."

"You didn't," I say, and this time I mean it. "You didn't cause any of it."

"I know," she says. "I mean, I *know* that. But it still feels awful. Like I borrowed excitement and handed you consequences."

That lands uncomfortably close to the truth, raw and exposed as a scraped knee.

"I'm sorry," she says again. Not dramatic. Just sincere. "I didn't think it through. I don't usually. I just...wanted something different for once."

I look toward the living room, toward the couch, toward the shadows where the white plastic basket is still tucked half out of sight. "Different has a way of sticking around longer than you expect," I say.

She lets out a breathy, humorless laugh. "Yeah. I'm starting to figure that out."

In the background, a dog barks—her retriever, if I remember right. She shushes it, laughter fraying at the edges.

We sit in silence for a moment, the line open between us. It's not awkward, just charged—a wire waiting for a spark.

"If you ever want coffee," she says finally. "Or just to talk to someone who won't pretend this was normal."

"I'll keep that in mind."

After we hang up, the house feels quieter, not calmer—just hollowed out, like something has shifted and isn't done shifting yet. I set the phone down and stare at it for a second longer than necessary, thumb tracing the faint ring from my last mug of tea.

Then I stand up.

That night, sleep still won't come. I give up and drag the white plastic laundry basket out from where I shoved it earlier. I spread the folders across the living room floor, the house quiet in that predawn hour where every sound—the hum of the fridge, the tick of the clock—feels too loud, invasive, insistent.

One by one, I open them. Manila paper rasps under my fingers, the powdery smell of old files making my nose itch. I type names into my laptop, keys clicking in the hush.

Seven folders, soft-edged from years of handling.

Seven men. Seven stories that stopped mid-sentence.

Every search ends the same way. Missing. No resolution.

No late-night "found safe." Different jobs. Different towns. Different lives. Nothing tying them together—except that each one vanished as if scrubbed clean from the world. I sit back on my heels, staring at the papers. The glow of the screen washes the room in sour, artificial light. The names line up like gravestones.

Jay didn't just disappear. He was erased.

And whatever he walked into, he wasn't the first.

I scroll again—slower this time—letting the search results breathe.

Joseph Taylor.

Not missing anymore. Recently identified. Found two years ago. A John Doe at first—pulled from a creek in a local park three counties over. They said he fell from the bridge. Said it might've been suicide. No note. No witnesses. Just water, concrete, and a file closed with a shrug.

Gabe Johnson.

Found in March. Drowned. Went out duck hunting alone and never came back. They called it an accident. Bad weather. Poor visibility. Another man who "should've known better."

Both of them were identified after the fact. Quietly. Tucked into databases like corrections, not conclusions.

I sit back, heart knocking slow and heavy now.

Missing men don't usually come back as accidents.

Not like that. Not one by one.

The others are still listed as unresolved. Still missing. Still waiting for a version of the truth that makes them easier to forget. Seven men. Two bodies.

One journalist who vanished before he could become the

third. Or maybe already dead. The pattern doesn't scream. It doesn't need to. It just waits—patient, deliberate—counting on people like me to look away when the story gets uncomfortable.

I don't.

I close the laptop and sit there in the dark, the house breathing around me, the folders spread out like a warning.

Whatever Jay uncovered wasn't meant to surface.

And now it has.

Chapter –11

Wednesday morning, they didn't let me inside. I stood in the parking lot as Shane walked through the doors of the placement facility, his duffel slung over one shoulder, posture stiff, bracing for impact. He didn't look back. I couldn't tell if that was courage, pride, or just self-preservation. The sound of the door thudded against the hush of morning, a hollow note in my ears.

I just wanted to be there for him—I know I wasn't supposed to be. But later that morning, Elle and Beth Ann stood on my porch, eyes tired but stubborn, trading looks full of silent plans. They'd jawed it up at the dollar store the night before, voices echoing over cheap linoleum and the rattle of the ancient HVAC. Neither of them thought it was right or fair. Elle had heard from Ryder where Shane was headed. She drove us to Simon Young Foster Youth Services, a long-term housing unit for teens, the car thick with nerves and the faint, burnt-sugar smell of spilled soda.

I finally understood defensive driving lessons when Elle hit ninety on a curve marked twenty—her white knuckles wrapped around the wheel, wide grin daring the world to blink first. My hands cramped from gripping the seat and dashboard, sweat slicking my palms. The air tasted like adrenaline and road dust. I swear I left a permanent scream in that car.

The building used to be an insurance office—you could tell. Beige brick, narrow windows, a flag out front snapping too loud in the wind. No bikes. No toys. No basketball hoops or soccer goals. Just rules baked into the concrete, the air inside smelling faintly of disinfectant and old coffee, stifling any hint of play.

The caseworker clomped out in bland, worn heels, a blazer over a blouse and blue skirt that looked issued, not chosen. She handed me a laminated sheet through the cracked car window, her nails tapping against the plastic—a little drumbeat of bureaucracy. Her breath clouded in the chilly air, mixing with the exhaust curling through the lot.

She knew exactly who I was. Didn't ask my name. Kept her voice careful and flat, a practiced neutrality. Someone had warned her I'd show up.

I'd called Ryder the night before and screamed into the phone for ten straight minutes before hanging up. I didn't let him get a word in edgewise.

Lights out at ten. Shoes by the door. Phones surrendered at intake. No leaving after dark. No visitors for forty-eight hours. Not a drop of warmth anywhere on the page—just a chill that stuck to my skin, colder than the night outside.

"Temporary assessment placement," she said, as if the phrase could soften the blow. "They'll evaluate educational options. Shane's age puts him at a crossroads."

A crossroads. That's what they call it when a kid slips out of the pipeline—when they don't know what box to shove him in next.

She went on, flipping pages. "College isn't always the right path. Some boys do better learning a trade. Structure. Predictability." Her voice made it sound like a diagnosis, not a choice.

"I'm sure his dad wants him to go to college," I muttered. "Shane, too."

She just stared at me—hard and measuring—like the decision isn't mine. Or maybe it is, and she's already decided I'll never see it through, considering I can barely keep a job.

"If you think I can't afford it, I'd find a way," I added. "Not by robbing a bank. Legally. Promise."

Her stare sharpened, slicing right through me.

I nodded. No use arguing. Still, the idea stuck under my ribs, prickly and raw.

Shane doesn't need redirection. He needs an anchor.

That night, the house felt hollow without him. The floorboards creaked too loudly. Annie asked where he was three times before bed. I told her the truth I was allowed: "He's staying somewhere else for a few days."

"Is he in trouble?" she asked.

"No," I said. "He's just... waiting." The word felt thin, stretched to breaking.

I didn't hear about the break-in until Thursday afternoon. I was perched in the corner bleachers, metal cold through my jeans, waiting for Shane to show up at tryouts.

It came sideways, the way bad news always does—through Ricky Bradley, blowing his whistle and rattling my skull as the boys' basketball team finished practice. Sweat and echoes hung in the gym's air. I could see why they needed Shane's height; every other boy looked like they'd been built from pizza crusts and late-night gaming marathons.

"Hey!" he called up, waving a palm—way too casual. "You

wouldn't know anything about a group of kids breaking into Pinehaven Middle School last night, would you?"

My stomach dropped as I clambered down the bleachers, trying to look graceful but knowing I looked like a dog climbing out of a tree—awkward, all elbows and regret, sneakers squeaking against the rubber floor.

He didn't accuse. Didn't need to. He watched my face change and sighed. "Don't panic," he said. "No real damage. They tripped a motion sensor, set off the alarm. Cops were there in minutes."

"And Shane?" I asked.

He hesitated.

"He was there," Ricky said. "Didn't break anything. Didn't steal anything. He followed some older boys out a window. I saw the video." He frowned. "I was surprised to see you here. You didn't show up this morning—or the day before—to run, so I asked the front desk. Margorie Betts told me what happened."

I closed my eyes, wishing I could blink away the whole mess. The gym's lights sputtered behind my eyelids, leaving ghostly afterimages.

"Second night in placement," Ricky added quietly. "That's when it usually happens." His voice was softer than the squeak of shoes on the court—almost lost in the echoing gym.

"What happens?" I asked.

"The realization," he said. "That the rules don't care who you are."

He spoke like he knew. It was the first time I'd seen Ricky's eyes soften. I never asked, but I remembered a couple months in high school when he'd vanished. Back then, we were just relieved. I never thought about what happened—though the rumors had a way of clinging, like damp clothes.

He told me they caught them all. Shane didn't run, didn't mouth off, didn't swing. According to Ricky, he just stood there, hands at his sides, jaw locked—like he'd already done the math and knew what came next.

"Don't try to break him out," Ricky said. For a second, I thought he meant it—then caught the ghost of a grin. "Maybe this is what he needs. Harsh reality. Scared straight."

"Ricky, he's already a scared kid whose dad never came home," I said. "He's spent the last six months trying to fix it— not breaking laws that would land him in jail. He doesn't need a detention center or to get tossed through the foster system. He has me and his sisters. Or he did, until your buddy Noah Ryder from high school screwed that up."

I paused, realizing I'd had a hand in the fallout too. I shouldn't have dragged the kids to work that night.

"I learned my lesson," I said. "It just takes time to rebuild their trust. For all I know, Shane thinks his dad just decided not to keep them and went looking for something better. He was starting to open up. That's when he said he wanted to play basketball."

I hesitated. "If I can get hold of the foster agency and they'll bring him down here, can he get a second chance?"

"I don't know if they'll let that happen," Ricky said. "Most kids don't come back to regular high school. They get shunted into job training programs."

"Yeah," I said. "I can see that." I swallowed. "They won't

even let me call him. I keep thinking if I could just talk to him—let him know I'm not mad he called Noah Ryder—I could change everything."

But I knew I couldn't. Because I was still burned that he had. Trying not to be. I'm a work in progress.

Shane called that night. I didn't ask how or why. His voice came through the phone cracked and watery—he burst into tears, rambling before I could get a word in.

"I'm sorry. I'm so, so sorry. I don't know why I told Ryder where we were. I was just texting him. And the school break-in—they were going anyway," he said. "I didn't plan it. I just… didn't stop it."

"I know," I said. Because I did. Shane wasn't a ringleader. He was a gravity well—pulled along by whatever force promised him a little control.

"They talked about trades again," he whispered. "Like college is a fairy tale."

I gripped the edge of the counter, knuckles white. "And what did you say?"

"That I just want to play basketball," he said, voice barely above a whisper. "Just once." I heard the longing threaded between the words, so thin it could snap.

I promised him I was working on it. But my hands were tied by an unforgiving system. It felt like captaining a sinking boat—tossing him a life jacket just as he jumped overboard. I knew he'd cling to it, cling to the idea of basketball, because it was the last dream he had left.

And even as I threw it, I realized the buckles were broken. Too loose. Too big. I'd given him something that looked like hope but wouldn't hold. Something he'd slip right out of, quietly, before anyone noticed he was drowning. Or maybe his head was already going under, and I was just standing on the shore, useless.

Before he hung up, the line turned deathly quiet. I had my window cracked open, cold air needling my skin. Pines crowded the forest behind the house, their scent drifting in— sharp and clean, like Christmas—calming in a way I didn't deserve. My fingertips stung. I didn't want to ask if he knew where his sisters were sleeping or if his bed was comfortable. I already knew the answers. I've never been good at small talk, not when the truth sits heavy and unmoving between us.

Finally, he let out a long sigh and asked the question that cinched my chest tight.

"Did you really talk to Dad the night he didn't come back?" His voice was careful, like he'd been holding the question in for days, afraid of what the answer might do. "Were you really going out with him again?"

I narrowed my eyes, shaking my head even though he couldn't see. "I hadn't seen your dad since you all moved away," I said, slow and careful. "Didn't even know you'd come back. So, no." I paused. "Where'd you get something like that?"

He didn't answer right away. I knew by the silence.

"Somebody found some notes and stuff," he said finally. "They said the cops have video of you two eating at a restaurant you used to go to. Somewhere by the beach."

My stomach plummeted, cold and hollow, as if I'd swallowed a stone. The beach. Or somewhere close to it.

Three Broke Moms Detective Agency

There was a little backwater diner we used to haunt along Cape Fear, not far from Wrightsville Beach—easy to miss if you didn't know where to look. Afterward, I'd walk the shoreline, especially in fall and winter, when the tourists vanished and the sand felt untouched—cool and gritty beneath my soles. I'd hold his hand, bend to pick up dented shells worn thin by the tide. For a few quiet minutes, it felt like we owned that stretch of beach. Like it belonged to us alone.

Back then.

"Why would they tell you that?" I asked carefully. "And who told you?"

Another pause.

"Ryder's been asking questions, Misty," he said. "I told him I didn't know anything. Maybe you should ask him. I don't trust him now." His voice cracked. "I'm sorry. I shouldn't have told him anything."

"There's nothing to tell," I said, and meant it. But even as I spoke, a cold awareness slid down my spine. Stories about me were moving through town—half-formed, reshaped, passed hand to hand like counterfeit bills, edges worn thin by too many retellings.

And I had the uneasy feeling those stories weren't done changing yet—a chill crawling up the back of my neck, promising more trouble on the horizon.

Chapter −12

Ryder's intentions set off alarms in my head. He's always coasted on good looks and charm—Pinehaven's favorite currency—but the small-town-boy shine has dulled, the cute, lopsided grin now practiced, worn thin like a mask that never quite fit.

Jenny Langstrom—my chemistry partner—used to laugh whenever I'd fake a gag at the sound of girls gossiping about him. Those laughing blue eyes, they'd sigh, dreamy, the deep brown hair adding some kind of halo to his head. Spellbound. Like he had them under glass, pinned and perfect.

I'd lean in and tell Jenny what I really thought: Ryder was the devil incarnate. Nobody's that good—not for free, not in a town like this. It had to be a mask for whatever simmered underneath—something patient, something mean.

Because I knew for a fact he wasn't just the golden boy Pinehaven wanted him to be.

He'd been one of those boys with Ricky Bradley, back behind the dugout—fists flying while that kid tried to curl into himself, small and silent. And Ryder... Ryder didn't stop it. I'm sure Billy Ramsey instigated the whole thing. Billy always was that ruthless, reckless troublemaker—the one flicking a lighter while strolling through a fireworks factory. He talked back to the principal, picked on little kids, and was meaner than a rattler you stepped on twice.

I know he was like that right up until the day he died in that fire.

And now his old best friend walks with a cane and a careful

voice, talking about "best interests," as though time and tragedy sanded him into something kinder.

I don't buy it. Not for a second.

Men don't wake up and grow a conscience overnight. They learn to wear one like a suit—pressed, borrowed, never quite belonging to them.

I'm staring at that mask right now, across the cramped office Ryder keeps in the back of the police station, its air thick with the sour tang of old coffee and disinfectant.

My left hand is knotted into a fist on his desk as I lean in, the wood cold against my knuckles. With the other, I keep pushing back my hair—frizzier than usual, a long mess I didn't have time to tie up this morning. Ryder just stares at me doing it, silent, unreadable. My right arm cradles a very angry Nacho—fur bristling, eyes wild and glassy—fresh from the pound and reeking of rubber gloves and fear. Suddenly, Nacho springs out of my arms and launches across the desk, scattering Ryder's paperwork everywhere. Ryder just picks him up, unbothered, like he's known the cat forever. Nacho purrs in his arms as Ryder hands him back—then promptly hisses at me.

"Can you explain to me"—I hiss, awkwardly shifting Nacho as he squirms and digs his claws into my forearm, my grip careful, like I'm holding a hot skillet ready to burn—"how Shane is better off, after being charged with breaking and entering and missing his basketball tryout?"

I don't even mention Billy—my brother, second-grade teacher at Pinecrest Elementary—how he stopped by the office yesterday to make copies and found Daisy sprawled on the floor, sobbing so hard she didn't move. How she went completely limp—full toddler shutdown—playing dead like a possum on linoleum.

She opened one eye just long enough to recognize Billy. The red hair. The freckles. Family.

He coaxed the story out of her between hiccupping breaths.

They'd placed her in Debby Boyer's foster home. Debby Boyer—who's allergic to cats. Debby Boyer—who owns three huskies. The dogs tried to eat Nacho, so Debby boxed him up and dumped him outside the dog shelter fence in the middle of the night like a sack of trash. I didn't find out until nine the next morning. By then, Nacho was gone. Only an empty box with the tape ripped off remained.

I missed work—spent six hours combing the neighborhood, setting out tuna cans as breadcrumbs, quarter mile by quarter mile, calling his name until my throat was raw. Found him eventually—mean, terrified, all claws and bone, unmistakably himself.

Ryder doesn't interrupt. He watches me from behind that desk, expression careful. Composed. Practiced. The fluorescent light above him flickers, making his eyes seem almost colorless.

That mask again. And I realize something, standing there with claw marks burning on my arms and a snarling cat digging into my jacket:

This isn't about procedure. It's about control. Ryder's always been comfortable deciding who gets it—and who doesn't.

"You were texting a juvenile under my care," I say, my voice low and sharp. "Asking him questions without my permission. An adult chatting with a kid? That's suspect. More than a little creepy."

"Texting? With Shane?" He sits up straighter, wide-eyed with innocence, as if the idea has never even crossed his mind.

"Yes. That's what he told me. And what's this about me meeting Jay Hensley the night he never came home? I didn't. I hadn't seen him in two years. It makes me look like I had something to do with his dad's disappearance. Why would you tell a child—whose father is missing—something like that?" I demand. "Unless you were trying to turn him against me."

I draw in a breath, steadying myself before he can answer. "This is all *your* fault. These kids were fine under my care. Not perfect—what family is?—but safe. Now Shane is going to have a record." I barrel on, not letting him interrupt. "And just so you know, you broke the law yourself a long time ago. I saw you with those boys at the ball diamond, beating up that kid. Don't think I didn't. You're not the only one who deserves a second chance. Just because Shane got stuck with me as a guardian doesn't mean he should have to pay for it."

I throw my hands up, words spilling faster now. "And Daisy's never going to trust an adult again, and—"

"Molly ran away this morning," Ryder says, his voice barely audible. "She didn't show up at school."

The room tilts. For the first time, his mask doesn't matter at all. Is Ryder telling the truth about texting Shane? The air tastes of panic—bright and bracing, like biting into a green apple—and my grip on Nacho tightens as everything unsaid presses in.

Chapter −13

Everyone looked where children are supposed to go.

The playground. The school. The woods behind the ballfield. A friend's house.

Police cruisers crawled past swing sets and cul-de-sacs, uniforms flashing between hedges and chain-link fences, checking all the places that made sense.

They never checked the one place that didn't. My house. No one thought to look where the system had already decided she didn't belong.

She's sitting on the back porch when I run back inside to put Nacho away—knees pulled to her chest, arms wrapped tight around them like she's bracing against a cold that isn't really there. I dump the cat inside and come back out, sitting beside her on the steps.

"I don't like it at Miss June's house," she says quietly. "She's got a bunch of little kids, and I have to share a room with them." She pauses. "They took my phone. She won't let me bring my trumpet home from school again. She yelled at me, said it sounded awful." To be fair to Miss June, it probably did sound awful. My brother played the drums his first year— let's just say the neighbors started wearing ear protection and our dog tried to run away twice.

"I'm sure Miss June just doesn't have an ear for good music," I say, feigning confidence like I'm not the one who once mistook the clarinet section for a flock of geese last time I went to a football game.

"Thank you for the trumpet," she says. "I really didn't think you'd get me one. Dad wouldn't. He said it was a waste of money, that most kids give up once the fun wears off." She keeps her eyes glued to the yard, not daring to look at me, like if she does, I'll send her packing. As if I ever could.

"You're welcome. The deal is, you have to keep playing until at least I've paid it off—which, at this rate, means you'll be serenading me at my retirement party." I don't tell her that'll really be about ten years, give or take a decade. But she huffs a drab laugh.

"She says I'll leave in a few days when they find somebody else to take me," Molly goes on, her voice flattening, like she's repeating something she's already practiced saying. "But it might be longer. Or they might have to try a few places. Move me around." She swallows. "She said people always want the little kids."

That part lands harder than anything else.

"I don't want to go back," she adds. "I'm worried about Daisy. And Shane. I've never been without them."

Then, softer—almost like she's testing the thought for the first time—"Maybe you don't want me."

She finally looks up.

"I like having you around," I say quickly. "Popcorn fights on the couch are boring without you. Annie just eats them like a dog."

She forces a small smile that doesn't stick.

"I didn't do anything wrong," she says. "I didn't tell on you—to that cop or that other guy. Not like Shane."

"You mean Noah Ryder?" I ask. "The one who came when they took you guys?"

"Well, him. But mostly that other cop." She shrugs. "Shane told him to stay away. He was afraid you'd be mad. The cop said he knew Ryder. Worked with him." She hesitates. "He gave Shane Ryder's information on a card."

"A card," I repeat. Too clean. Too intentional.

"He tried to talk to us at the dollar store the other day," she adds. "But he was creepy."

"He was wearing a police uniform?" I ask. "Was he with Ryder?"

"No. He said he was off-duty. Just saw us and wanted to say hi. Give us Ryder's card."

"Do you still have that card?"

She grimaces. "I threw it away."

Twenty minutes later, with garbage scattered across the yard, I'm holding a business card with Ryder's name on it.

I don't call the number. I look it up.

Nothing. No listing. No address. Just a name and a phone number hanging in the air like a bad smell. I know what I have to do. I don't want to do it.

I call Ryder anyway, half-expecting him not to answer once he sees my name. He does.

"Two things," I say. "First—I found Molly. She's safe. Second, is this your phone number?"

I read the number off the card.

There's a pause on the other end. Then he clears his throat. "No," he says. "Why?"

"Because that's the number Shane's been talking to," I tell

him. "Your name is on the card. No address. No other information. Molly and Shane were given those cards at the dollar store."

Silence.

"The guy said he worked with you," I add. "I knew that was a lie the second he said you were a cop. So—were you really texting Shane for the last few days?" I don't soften it. "Don't lie to me, or I'll find that pitching machine, drag it to your house, and launch it again."

I swear I hear a chuckle on the other end before it's stifled. "I did not text Shane."

"Then how did you know I was at the park?"

"I got a text from Molly," he says. "Said you threatened to hit her in the car. That you were beating up on Shane."

"Hold that thought," I say, pushing open the back door and slipping into the kitchen.

I keep my voice even. "I'm just going to ask. You're not in trouble." I meet her eyes. "Did you text Ryder and tell him I was hitting you guys?"

Molly tips her head sideways, lips curling like I just told the flattest joke she's ever heard.

"You? Hit us?" she says. "Misty, you pick up every worm on the sidewalk so nobody steps on them. No. Why would I do that?"

"I don't know," I say. "Maybe so you didn't have to do chores. Or you didn't like my fried chicken. Or you hated staying here." I shrug. "I'm not exactly rich. I can't buy you stuff all the time."

"No," she says immediately. "I felt safe here."

Her eyes don't dart away. No hesitation. No earlobe tug—the old tell she's had since she was little, back when she'd sneak cookies before supper.

I go back outside and sit on the step, phone still pressed to my ear.

"Ryder," I say quietly. The yard feels suddenly too still. "Can you get in touch with the police and find out where Shane and Molly's phones are now—and who's been calling them? Molly says she never texted you." I draw a breath. "I understand you didn't hear this directly from her. But you also didn't hear it directly from her that I hit her. It was a text. Did anyone check the cell phone number of the call? Barring real emergencies—the guy at the park, you with the baseball pitching machine—I don't swing at adults unless they're hurting someone else. And I would never hit a kid. Not even under duress."

I sit there for a second after hanging up, phone warm in my hand, the yard gone too quiet—like the crickets are holding their breath.

Molly never texted him. Ryder didn't text Shane.

And somebody went to the trouble of printing cards with Ryder's name on them, handing them to kids, and planting just enough fear to get the system to do the rest.

That isn't coincidence. That's rehearsal.

I look toward the street, toward town—toward the dollar store with its humming lights and quiet cameras and aisles everyone forgets once they leave. Someone talked to Jay's kids. Tomorrow, I'm going to find out who.

Chapter −14

Ricky waited outside the school office, hands jammed in his pockets, jaw clenched so tight I could almost hear his teeth grind. He said little, and I didn't push—except for the one thing that mattered.

He told me it was Ryder who'd quietly set everything in motion—calling the station, pushing for an emergency meeting with Children's Services, spinning concern into something that looked like control.

In Pinehaven, names still mattered, and Ricky's dad mattered most of all. A judge's phone call. A few pointed questions. Just enough pressure to make Children's Services slow down, to make them actually look at what they'd rushed to finish.

But the phones told a story no one wanted to hear.

Those texts threatening abuse? They hadn't come from Molly. Or Shane. Or Daisy. Not from any number tied to the kids, period. Someone had run them through a masking service—just convincing enough to fool a quick glance, just brittle enough to shatter under real scrutiny. Once that was clear, everything shifted: no charges, no formal findings. Just clipped phrases—"unsubstantiated," "administrative error," "children returned to guardian pending review."

By dinner, all three kids were back in the house—Daisy curled against Annie on the couch. Shane was home from the teen placement unit, too—quiet, watchful, like he didn't trust the floor to stay under him. Molly was quiet but anchored at my side, her shoulder solid and warm against mine. Nacho reclaimed his throne on Daisy's lap, a king returned to his kingdom, tail swishing with royal satisfaction.

But this time, everyone was actually eating. I watched them—forks moving, food disappearing. And for a second, I flashed back to those first nights: me baking chocolate chip cookies at two a.m., desperate for something they'd trust. Next morning, peanut butter and jelly. Pizza pockets after school. Chocolate milk with extra syrup. Every comfort I could think of, just to get them to take a bite.

Shane caught my eye and grinned. "Hey, Daisy, Molly—remember when Misty thought cookies and pizza would fix everything? If you two just poke at your food like before, she'll probably let us have brownies for breakfast."

Molly rolled her eyes, but she was chewing. "Don't tempt me."

Daisy snorted. "Nuh uh. That lady where I stayed cooked so bad it tasted like Nacho's cat food."

I didn't ask how she knew what Nacho's food tasted like.

Shane made a face. "See?" he teased. "That's probably why this happened. It's a total Misty move—teaching us a lesson hands-on, so she doesn't have to ground us to our rooms and be stuck at home. Now she's got us trained."

Annie nudged Daisy gently, and Nacho—sensing the mood—thumped his tail against the table leg. For a moment, the room felt whole.

"I'm glad you all can kid about it. It was traumatic for me," I mutter, then poke a fork toward Shane. "I thought for sure I'd have to do your chores—taking out the trash and cleaning off the dishes."

"You still can."

"Nope."

Relief pricked at my neck, edged with something raw and unfinished.

It hummed under my skin, sharp and uneasy—a warning I couldn't shake.

Someone had forced the system to tear us apart. The system doesn't panic; people do.

Whoever did this knew where to press and how hard. If they went this far, what else might they try?

Chapter −15

By the time the school bell rings, I've already made three decisions that won't show on anyone's attendance sheet.

None of them involves permission. They involve boundaries, footage, and a name I don't trust.

That morning, after dropping the kids at school, I linger in the parking lot. The engine ticks, air sharp with the promise of rain. Normally, I'd be running the trail with Ricky—still keeping up, still pretending I don't care who wins our unofficial race. But he took the morning off for an early teacher's meeting.

I hate to admit it, but I'm starting to like running. As much as I stay quiet, I've come to appreciate Ricky's company—his running commentary on every botched play, every kid he's coaching, every time he nearly pulled a muscle. He talks with his whole body, hands slicing the air like he's pitching to an invisible crowd. Some mornings, that's enough to make me forget how much I feel alone.

I watch them disappear—Shane, tall and trying not to look back; Molly, feigning indifference but glancing sideways; Daisy, knuckles white around her backpack like it might float off if she lets go.

I squint after her, second-guessing myself. I caught her this morning trying to stuff old, fat Nacho inside her backpack, but the pack isn't moving—and with a cat that size, it would be scraping the ground by now.

I wanted to look professional today. And a little vintage. So I dug into my closet for what I call my mom-is-a-librarian outfit—a sweet floral print, slightly ditzy, the hem landing just above the knee. Modest heels give it a professional edge without trying too hard. I slide on my old glasses and twist my hair back, smoothing it straight while it still cooperates.

That will last until I hit any moisture between here and the coast. Less than ten miles inland from the coast, my hair will be sticking up like a clown in a horror movie, signaling distress long before I do. But by then, it won't matter. I only have one more stop to make on my way back—Wally needs me to pick up some files from the police station.

I still don't think they know I do surveillance work for him. He's convinced them I'm just office staff—home filing, data entry, the boring stuff. My little mishap at the soccer fields was chalked up as a miscommunication, and what I think he told the cops was "that ditzy redhead being a redhead again." Sometimes his stereotyping works in my favor.

For now, I look like someone who belongs exactly where she's headed. Wally calls it "playing investigator." I call it dressing for the answers I want.

Only when the doors swallow their voices and the echo of lockers clatters shut behind them do I turn toward the office.

I give myself one last look, smooth the skirt, and step out. The car door clicks shut behind me, loud in the morning hush.

The principal's door yawns open. I don't sit.

"I need to make something clear," I say, keeping my voice level—the only way people listen. "No one is to speak to Shane, Molly, or Daisy without my permission. Not the police. Not social workers. Not anyone 'just stopping by.'"

She blinks, then nods slowly, fingers already reaching for a yellow sticky note. The faint scent of coffee and lemon cleaner lingers in the air.

"I'll flag their files," she says. "Anyone who asks for access goes through you first."

Relief settles low in my chest—not peace, exactly, but a wary comfort, like building a fence and pressing your palms to it, half-expecting it to break. A boundary drawn in ink, not hope—a small, stubborn defense in a world full of fractures.

Only after I secure the principal's promise do I get back in the car, shift into drive, and press the gas pedal with tense hands, my knuckles turning pale on the steering wheel as I set my course for the dollar store.

Because whoever thought it was a good idea to hand my kids a business card and lie about who they worked for made one mistake. They did it somewhere with cameras—and I can feel the slow thump of my heartbeat as I reach for that one thread that might lead us out of this trap.

I wait in line longer than I need to—twenty minutes, counting the flickering fluorescent lights and the sticky ring of pine-scented floor wax. When the bell over the door finally goes still, I plop a single piece of wintergreen gum on the counter. Beth Ann's seen me in so many outfits over the years: coming and going from work, from school events, from rushed errands. She barely notices when I'm out of character.

"I got the kids back—"

Beth Ann's face lights up. She breaks into a little bounce behind the register, clapping once. "Yes!"

"—but," I add, lowering my voice, "I need some information."

She freezes mid-celebration.

I wink. "I'm looking for a source who can provide it."

Her hand reaches for the gum. I shake my head. "Uh-uh. Not until you spill."

"That won't get you far," she says, smirking.

I tip my chin, dig into my purse, and pull out a fresh pack. I slide two more pieces onto the counter, wiggling them like poker chips, the cellophane crinkling between my fingers.

"Hmmm." She extends two perfectly manicured fingers—cherry red with tiny white polka dots—presses them into the gum, sliding them to her side of the register. "What you need, sista?" She grins. "All the drama came through here this week. Want to hear about the three bottles of wine John Young bought yesterday? Or the pickles that vanished under a pregnant girl's coat? What's the scoop?"

"I need the videos from last week," I say. "The days my kids were here."

"Oh." Her grin softens, not quite disappearing. "Why?"

"Because a man talked to them," I say, voice barely above a whisper as I glance at the front windows. Leaning in, I lower my voice further. "He said he was a cop. Gave them a fake business card with Noah Ryder's name on it. Then he texted them, pretending to be Ryder. That's what started this whole mess."

Her eyes widen. "Oh my gosh."

"The police haven't been by asking for footage yet?"

She shakes her head, already reaching for my sleeve. "No. Not that I know of. Come on." Her nails are cool through my sleeve, a little tremor betraying her excitement.

She pulls me into a dim little room behind the counter. "Boss's office," she whispers. "He's cheap—just keeps the system running. I set it up straight out of the box two years ago, back when someone kept stealing milk and bread." She rolls her eyes. "He makes me review it once a week. It's mind-numbing."

She gestures at shelves lining the wall, stacked with dusty hard drives. "He keeps everything. I've got footage back to the dawn of time."

The front door chimes—a shrill, metallic note that scrapes up my spine.

Beth Ann sighs, the sound heavy as disappointment. "I can't do it now. But as soon as I get off, I'll check the feeds and pull stills. If he talked to your kids, he's on there." Her support warms the cold knot in my chest, a promise stronger than the lock on the door.

"I'll owe you," I say—my voice small, gratitude scraping at the edge of tears as I let the words settle between us, as firm and real as the hope I fight to hold onto.

She snorts. "You paid in gum." Her gaze skims over my outfit, maybe noticing for the first time that I might do more than tap at a computer all day. "Where are you going today? Got another case?"

"Wouldn't you like to know?" I tip my head, letting a sly smile bloom. She would. I see it—the longing in her eyes to ditch the register, spread her wings, and fly. "Maybe when you're off next time, I'll take you along. Two broke moms out playing detective."

Back out front, I check the clock: 8:30 a.m. The air tastes of wet asphalt and stale coffee drifting from the breakroom vent.

I have just under six hours before I need to be anywhere else—plenty of time to drive out to the Old Driftwood Bar and Grill.

Plenty of time to find out whether someone went digging for footage of Jay and me.

Because if someone was already rewriting our story, then this wasn't the beginning.

It was the part where I finally noticed.

Chapter –16

The Old Driftwood Bar and Grill doesn't look any different.

Same weathered sign. Same uneven planks on the porch. Same chalkboard menu, the *E* (it used to be Grille) half-erased, stubbornly refusing to disappear. The place wears years of storms and blistering summers—sagging just off the road like an old man too tired to go any further. I don't tell anyone who I am. I don't ask about Jay. Not yet.

I slip into my old booth by the window—where morning light spills in sideways and dust motes drift like lazy ghosts. Coffee, black. No rush. The walls crowd close with memory: For ten bucks, they'd take a Polaroid and tack it up on the wall—crooked grins, scribbled notes, dollar bills pinned with names and dates. Small, stubborn proof that someone passed through and left a mark.

Over the kitchen, a massive slab of driftwood splits the room—IF THE WALLS COULD TALK scorched into it in jagged letters.

That's why I always loved this place. It doesn't try—doesn't need—to be themed. It just is. Lived in. Loved. The building remembers things people can't, holding onto faces and voices long after we're gone. I was never truly a local, but the Driftwood made me feel like one. Jay and I were here so often, folks started waving before we even sat down—like they expected us, like we belonged.

You can always tell the regulars by the way they argue with the jukebox. Once, it swallowed someone's quarter and played Patsy Cline on a loop for three hours. People started betting on how long it'd last before breaking the spell. Nobody ever won. The owner came out, kicked it with his foot, and another song finally rolled out to a chorus of groans and mock applause. Someone claimed the jukebox had taste; someone else accused it of holding grudges. Even the tourists kept their distance, like it might bite.

It's that kind of place—where a machine can have an attitude, and everyone's in on the joke except the newcomers.

The waitress brings my coffee without a word, her hand practiced, her eyes unreadable. Perfect—I don't want to be noticed yet. A briny tang lingers in the air—shrimp shells, homemade bread, a ghost of hot sauce. The tabletop sticks to my forearm, tacky with old spills and salt.

This place holds memory the way old wood walls soak up stories and smoke—never letting go.

Jay and I used to haunt this place in the off-season, when the tourists vanished and the ocean hushed. We'd sit for hours, splitting greasy sweet potato fries, watching storms muscle their way in off the water. He'd trace the grain of the table, spinning stories about work as if it wasn't devouring him. Those were the days when anything felt possible—even for a girl with a colicky baby and nowhere to go. Back then, this was a kind of heaven.

I order the usual: fish sandwich, mountain of sweet potato fries, slaw, extra lemon. I wait. Patience is my secret talent— the kind that makes people underestimate you.

A couple at the next table is locked in an epic silent battle over the last onion ring. She nudges the plate halfway, staring him down. He cracks, splits it, and they both laugh—a ritual rehearsed a hundred times. I nearly smile. Some things never change.

The waitress returns, lingers a second longer. Her gaze skims over my glasses, my dress, the way I sit like I belong—even if I haven't in years. Something shifts: recognition, or maybe nostalgia.

"Been a minute." Her voice is careful. "I remember you."

I smile, easy. "Feels like it. Yeah—been a long time."

She nods. "You want your fries crispy, like before?" She glances at the door—expecting Jay, maybe. He doesn't appear. Her eyebrow arches, sharp as a question mark.

"Crispy," I say. "Always."

"You're alone this time, huh?"

"Yep. Just me and the old memories."

That does it. I let the silence stretch, wide as low tide. People always fill it sooner or later.

"He didn't talk much," she adds. "But he listened. Real polite. Always paid cash."

I stir my coffee. "Yeah?"

She nods. "I wondered when he came in alone one time—where you were. Sat right there." She points at the booth across from mine. "Didn't eat much. Just picked at it. Kept looking at the door. Like you, right now."

"Like me right now." I huff a laugh, but my hand stills on the mug. I don't ask when. I don't ask why.

I let her keep going. "Then there was another time," she says, frowning like she's about to step on glass. "Different woman. Hair nearly your color, a shade darker. I thought it was you, at first. But it wasn't. She didn't order the large fries."

She laughs, low and wry. "Not as sweet. Louder. They argued a little—not badly, just enough that folks started watching."

"When?" I ask. She probably thinks I'm jealous.

"May or June. It was hot, I remember that."

That's enough. She starts to walk away before I can say anything else, already regretting how much she's said. Then she turns, pokes a finger over my head. I twist in the booth. "They left a picture. Don't know if you want to see it. Figured you would, eventually."

I'm not sure I ever truly fell in love with Jay. Maybe I just loved this place with him—no crying baby, no parents judging, no work. Just fries and the illusion of possibility. Maybe it wasn't the same for him. I kneel on the booth for a better look at the photo. She's like me, but shorter, face pinched, hair dyed the color of cherry soda, eyes blue and a little startled. They're grinning too wide. Maybe he came here looking for a new me—someone easier to love, or just different. I snap a few photos on my phone.

There's a date scrawled in black marker at the bottom of the Polaroid: June 11. This year. Two days before he stopped answering his phone.

To the right: R.J. and J.H. Jay Hensley—and who? R.J.? Rhianna Johnson? Ruby Jenson? The walls seem to watch—patient, knowing—like they remember what people are desperate to forget.

Chapter –17

I stop at the police station on the way back. The lobby always carries the faint, medicinal tang of floor cleaner and old coffee, with a trace of day-old bologna sandwiches and something burnt clinging to the vents—like someone microwaved popcorn a week ago and nobody's owned up to it.

Files—nothing dramatic. No questions, no confrontation. I smile, I sign, I thank them for their time; a quick, practiced exit.

They still think I'm office help—data entry, filing, public information pulls for Wally. The harmless middle layer nobody worries about. That's fine; people talk when they think you don't matter.

I tuck the folder under my arm, the edges rough and thick beneath my fingers, already planning my exit into the late afternoon light. My reflection flashes in the glass: floral dress, sensible heels, old glasses catching the sun. I almost make it.

Then I catch the eye of the Pinehaven Chief of Police Daniel Mercer sitting behind his desk in the glass-walled office off the main floor. He's slightly stocky—muscled arms fill out his sleeves, broad shoulders hinting he still lifts, even if only for habit. Unlike the other hotdog-haired men orbiting him, his hair is clipped short, practical. A laid-back button-down, khakis, and a thick binder open on his desk complete the scene.

The chief running Pinehaven now wasn't the man I'd worked under. The old chief retired quietly, but his way of running the precinct lingered. The new chief was younger, yet still bound to rules that belonged to another century.

Chief Mercer hadn't been there when I started missing shifts because Jay's kids needed someone and there wasn't anyone else. When I was told to choose between showing up like nothing was wrong or admitting that something was.

I didn't really have a choice.

The chief changed. The tone didn't. And the men who learned the old rules were still enforcing them.

Chief Mercer barely looks up.

With one hand still resting on the binder, he lifts the other and jerks his thumb toward the back hallway. "Go talk to Noah Ryder."

I want to whine like Annie does when she dreads a bedtime bath. I don't.

I bob my head and give him a geeky thumbs-up instead, already turning down the hall like this was always part of the plan.

"The chief said I needed to see you, Ryder?" I ask, standing just inside the doorway, taking in the room piece by piece. "What is your job, anyway?"

His desk is buried in paper—mounds a foot high, files bleeding into one another as if he's got a hand in everything, wanted or not. No photos. No kids. No family. Not even a curling snapshot of parents or a forgotten holiday.

The walls are bare, washed in a tired yellow that looks like it gave up trying to be cheerful years ago. A lone laptop sits on the desk beside a stapler, three half-empty coffee cups, and a humming printer shoved just close enough to be useful.

It's the kind of space that says someone's been here too long and doesn't expect anyone to notice—or care.

I must have startled him. His face is hard-set at the screen, fingers tapping fast, focused. When he looks up, his gaze lands on me with the drowsy calm of a gazelle at a pond—right before it realizes the cheetah is airborne. My hair's probably a frizzy mess from the drive. No wonder I look alarming.

He jerks to his feet, bangs into the desk, blinks hard, and spills coffee across his pants and the cluttered desktop. The laptop wobbles. He sucks in a sharp breath, bracing for impact.

"Boo?" I tease, trying to break the tension.

He recovers quickly. Too quickly. He tries to fool me with a smile—some might call it brave, or wistful. But I know the look: worn smooth by surrender, polished until it almost passes for pride.

"Uh. My official title is Administrative Specialist-County Liaison," he says. "Unofficially? Grunt."

I poke a finger at one of the paper piles. "Am I in one of these?" I ask, kidding. Mostly.

"With your record? Probably most of them."

My gaze darts up.

He's already working up a grin. "I'm just kidding," he adds. "Unless you know something I don't?"

"I'm just a little jumpy after this week's spectacular, egregious catastrophe."

He blinks. "Egregious?"

"That's what Molly called it," I say. "She's into words I have to translate on my phone now. It gives her time to run before I figure out she's just called me a danger to society. They all think it's hilarious. It's wild how hard it is to look up words fast. I almost wish she'd try Japanese—at least then the translation's obvious. Sometimes I think kids today are smarter than we ever were."

He actually laughs—quiet, surprised, like the sound escapes before he can stop it. More than I've ever heard him say at once. We never ran in the same circles. I was a math-club geek. He was into—besides sports, I couldn't tell you.

Noah fumbles for a pen in his shirt pocket, but instead pulls out a crumpled fortune cookie wrapper. He stares at it, annoyed, and tosses it onto the pile of paperwork. He tries again, this time producing a pen, but it explodes—blue ink splattering across his hand and a few official forms. He wipes his hand on a napkin, only managing to smear the ink further, leaving a streak across his cheek. He notices me watching, jaw tight, but doesn't comment. For a second, his calm slips, and I see the boy who once panicked at a pop quiz—just before he smooths his face out again, all business.

"I'm supposed to apologize," he says finally. "Per Judge Bradley and about six agencies that I think they invented just to give relatives jobs." He scoots in his seat, looking everywhere but at me. "I am sorry—" he starts, then grinds his teeth hard. His fingers tap on the desk. TAP-TAP-TAP.

"I'm sorry, I didn't hear that?" I say, leaning in. "Can you say it louder?" I cup a hand behind my ear. "Is it an apology I hear coming so I can do a victory dance?"

I hug the papers in one arm and perform a shameless jig, swinging the other in a full, triumphant circle.

He's not amused, though I grin. His jaw works, teeth grinding—he's the type who never thinks he's wrong, never owes an apology.

"I said," he repeats, louder, voice catching, "I am sorry—" Then he stops, stands again, fingers tapping. "I'm sorry I jumped on it, in some ways. In others, I'm not. I was trying to protect those kids. I knew you. I didn't think you'd hurt them, but I had to choose. They said you were hitting them. I took the risk and protected them. I—"

"That's fair." I shrug.

He freezes. "It is?"

I shrug again. "Your kind of work usually sees the worst side of people. You don't know me."

"Yeah," he says slowly. "Didn't have much to go by—except for the scar you gave me in high school with that pitching machine." He rubs his shoulder, almost fondly.

"And I made a quick, risky choice back then, too," I say. "Mine was just more satisfying though. We're even."

My eyes dart to the clock. Half an hour to pick up Shane and Molly before beating the bus home for the girls. The older two would never mar their reputation by taking the bus. They threatened to walk, but I'm not quite sure about them strolling the sidewalks alone yet.

"I've got to get the kids. Do I need to sign anything? A waiver? A note to your boss saying you sort-of apologized?" He bites his lip—my words steer us south again. "I'm kidding. I do that when I don't want to be somewhere I already am."

He looks past me, checking the hall, then lowers his voice. "Are the kids okay?"

"As good as they can be," I say. "Considering their dad is missing. And the police are working on that." I lie—I'm putting in more hours than they ever have.

"It didn't mess them up, right? The—"

"Misunderstanding?" I cut in. "I don't know, Noah. Missing the basketball tryout with Coach Bradley was a big deal. One I'm still trying to fix. Maybe you could come over and shoot baskets with him sometime—so he doesn't think the whole system's broken. Out of all the foster families, it felt like they were scraping the bottom of the barrel."

And I don't think that was accidental. I know there are good ones around.

He nods, uncertain. He's probably been told not to go within a ten-mile radius of us by now.

I turn to leave, give him a nod, and break into another victory dance while he's wiping off his desk. Nobody talked about who printed the cards or spoofed the texts—just reports, timestamps, and whether I'd made them look bad.

"Nice, Misty," he mutters.

But when I glance back, he's smiling.

~

By the time I settle the kids in after school, the sun's already slipping low, stretching the yard in gold and shadow. The air is cooler than I expect—tinged with cut grass, with a sharpness that tastes like rain even if the sky's clear. Somewhere down the hall, Molly runs the same three notes again, louder this time.

I hear a car in the drive and I walk to the door, listening to steps patter outside as I open it. Not loud. Not urgent. Just... certain. Beth Ann stands there when I open it ajar, her phone in hand, breath hitching like she ran the whole way.

"I got off early," she says. "And I looked." She chews her gum hard, jaw working, then blows a dull green bubble—chew, chew, blow, pop, inhale. This time, she snaps through the ritual twice in quick succession, as if her nerves need the distraction.

She turns the screen toward me. "Thought you'd want to see this."

And I know—before I even look—that whatever's on that phone is about to change everything.

Chapter −18

Beth Ann is nearly panting, cheeks flushed and sticky with sweat. The phone is clammy in her grip as she thrusts it between us, like it might bite—her hand trembling, the faintest click of her nail against the plastic. I smell something sharp and citrusy from her perfume.

I lean in, my elbow bumping the knob, the screen's glow painting Beth Ann's face ghostly pale. The photo's grainy, off-kilter; the man is caught mid-step, his posture hunched, average height vanishing into anonymity. A mop of gray-brown hair blurs at his temple, and thick glasses glint. His blue jacket is zipped halfway, collar wrinkled and flattened, like someone's fist has wrung it out. The faint hum of the kids in the other room undercuts the hush between us.

"It looks like that guy from the county paper last week," Beth Ann says, snapping her fingers in rapid staccato, as if the rhythm might knock the name loose. "They gave out those free grants to people in the county. He's got those huge teeth—mouth always open when he grins. I know it's him."

I lean back, phone already in hand, the screen warm against my palm. The local paper's site loads slow, choked with bake sales and weather alerts. The faint tap of my thumb on glass is the only sound for a moment. Then—there he is. Grinning wide, teeth bared, arms full of oversized checks. A group of people crowds around, their smiles stretched too tight, eyes darting off-camera. The image pixelates when I zoom, the faces smearing into colored static.

Mom had fumed when she saw that article. Thousand-dollar grants handed out like Halloween candy—to friends, to family. People they wanted to influence. Money that should've gone to the parks, the fields, the places meant to draw people in instead of quietly rotting under sun and wind.

"This guy?" I shove the phone toward her. "Tyler Maxwell?"

"Oh my gosh. Yes." She hisses, snapping her gum so hard it cracks. Her jaw works, chewing through a problem. She pauses, chin tipping sideways. "Why would he do this?" she asks. "Everybody knows him. The kids could recognize him."

I can see the answer settle over her as she reads my face.

My stomach knots, sour and twisting, the pressure like a fist pressing beneath my ribs. Sweat beads at the back of my neck, and I sigh so deeply, it makes me dizzy.

Nobody would believe us. Not after the foster care mess. Not after they twisted everything, made me look unstable just for trying to help Kylie. It had all felt so carefully arranged. Staring at the photo now, I see how easily he could deny it. Say it wasn't him. Say someone else handed out the cards. Say the kids were confused.

Looking like that, he could pass for three other men in this town—faces blurred by routine, details forgotten by everyone but us.

Once I said "fake cop," I wouldn't get control back.

"Keep this quiet for a few days," I murmur. "I don't know where to take it yet. Need to dig a little first."

Is it all connected? Or just a coincidence—Tyler Maxwell acting like some creep who thought he could scare kids into silence? No. There are too many lines crossing here. The red-haired woman Jay was seen with. The seven men who vanished before Jay. The timing. The cards. "We can't let them know we know it's him," I add. "Not yet. Whoever—or whatever—is running this."

Beth Ann nods, mouth set in a hard line—the humor gone, just grit left.

I glance over her shoulder. Her kids are bobbing in the back seat of her car, silhouettes shifting and smearing against the glass as they wrestle for space. Their laughter vibrates off the glass, a muffled thud. One of them thumps a sneaker against the door. "You guys eaten supper yet?" I ask, raising my voice so it cuts past Daisy screaming happily.

She shakes her head.

"How about you all eat over here tonight?" I offer. "I want to show you something."

My phone buzzes. I'm so focused on Beth Ann that I hesitate before answering, thumb hovering like I'm already tired of whoever it is.

"Hey—are you running tomorrow or not?" Ricky says without preamble.

Before I can answer, he grunts. "Your boyfriend called and shamed me into giving that Hensley kid another try. Tomorrow after school. Last chance."

"My boyfriend?" I repeat.

Ricky snorts. "Relax. Ryder. He was up my—" he cuts himself off, "—about that *tall* kid with the brown hair who just started school. Said he's been through enough."

"Oh. Okay," I say, still processing.

He's already halfway gone. The line crackles. "Be there."

The call drops just as I say, a beat too late—

"My *boyfriend*?"

I stare at the phone like it might explain itself. Then I hold up a finger at Beth Ann—one second—and hurry inside and down the hall, stopping just outside Shane's room.

"Hey!" I call over the clatter of keys and game noise. "Coach Bradley's giving you another shot!"

There's a beat of stunned silence. Then Shane's chair scrapes back hard enough to thump the wall. "What?"

"Tomorrow after school," I say. "Last chance."

The door cracks open. For the past hour, Molly's been practicing her trumpet inside—every off-key blast ricocheting off the walls, burrowing deep into my nerves until I'm convinced I can taste brass. Her face appears first, eyes wide, hope flaring before she can school it back into place. Then, like a magician revealing her best trick, she swings the trumpet into view and lets out a triumphant blare that rattles the windowpanes. From behind her, Daisy gasps. Annie cheers like someone just won the lottery and she's already spending her cut.

Shane bursts into the hallway, disbelief written all over him. "You're serious?"

"Completely," I say. "So don't blow it. Be there."

He grins—wide and reckless—and disappears back into his room like if he stops moving, the chance might evaporate. I know he's grabbing his basketball, going to shoot it way past the time I turn on the driveway lights. I stand there a moment longer than I mean to, listening to the house fill with noise again. Laughter. Arguing. Life is pushing back in where fear had been.

When I return to the front porch, Beth Ann is watching me quietly. "That matters," she says.

"Yeah," I reply. "It does."

I push the door open wider. "Get them inside."

And for the first time all day, I feel it—just a trace of ground under my feet. Not safety. Not answers.

But momentum. Whatever's circling us hasn't won yet.

And tomorrow, at least, one good thing is still possible.

The kids dive into frozen pizza, steam curling off the cheese, the crust crisping in their hands. Grease slicks their fingers as they eat like it's a delicacy they've never tasted, even though they had it twice last week. Shane and Dallas know each other from gym and algebra; they vanish into his room, plates clattering, the thump of hurried footsteps and the slap of game controllers against the desk echoing through the hall. Molly and Shenandoah, just a year apart, turn on a sitcom— canned laughter mixing with their giggles. Daisy and Annie sprawl on the floor, crayons rolling under the table, the waxy scent mingling with pepperoni and pizza.

I keep the basket shoved under the sink where it's been hiding, like it knows it's dangerous. Instead, I slide my phone across to her—screenshots, names, dates. The kind of information that looks harmless until you stack it.

"I can't tell you where I got them," I say. "Not yet. But I need you to help me run these names." I lower my voice. "Just... trust me. I think they're connected to Jay." I let out a slow breath. "No direct link, though. Just that they're missing. Like Jay. Two are dead."

I turn, rubbing my forehead. My skin feels clammy under my palm. "I've dug deep—mostly social media. Families still looking, heartbreak anniversaries, photos lit by candlelight, prayer requests. Nothing official."

"Did you check NamUs?" Beth Ann asks.

I pause, studying her face for a sparkle of something—fear, memory, hope.

"You know about NamUs?"

She nods. "Yeah. My uncle vanished when I was a kid. That's how we found out about it." She shrugs—casual, but her voice goes thin. "The national missing persons database."

I glance toward the kids' laughter tumbling down the hall. "No," I admit. "Didn't have time. This all landed in my lap, then everything with the kids happened. I haven't had space to dig in until now."

"I'll do it," she says, almost before I finish. "If you make copies, I'll start tonight. There has to be a connection somewhere."

"Or it's a wild goose chase," I say, but I'm already pulling out my phone.

I scroll to the photos from the restaurant—Jay and the woman sitting too close, both of them smiling too wide. "This used to be our favorite spot," I say, voice low. "He brought her back there right before he vanished." My hands are cold and tacky against the phone as I pass it to Beth Ann. The scent of fried onions and old coffee lingers in the memory of the place, curling up at the edges of the photo.

She studies it, eyes narrowing. "Your doppelgänger," she whispers, lips quirking. Then she looks up, grinning. "You're much prettier, of course."

I snort. "Eight missing men—including Jay. Two confirmed dead. And someone's trying to set me and the kids up." I chew my lip, thinking. "So... when are you off next? When the kids are at school?"

"I can call in sick tomorrow," she says, not missing a beat.

I nod slowly. "How about I try to get back into the Hensley house"—I hook my fingers in air quotes—"to 'pick up some clothes.' We'll see if Jay left anything else behind."

Chapter –19

Beth Ann texted me just after nine.

She found John Garcia, one of the men in the folders.

Age thirty-four. Five foot nine. One hundred thirty-eight pounds. Dark hair. Brown eyes. One minute alive, the next, dead. They found him last September near the Second Street Pier in Myrtle Beach—drowned, no foul play suspected. He haunted the beach at night, a solitary swimmer. Worked for Great Perks Global Travel Reservation Systems.

No close family. It took weeks to identify him. The body remains unclaimed, drifting between forms and signatures, as if waiting for someone to remember. The photo she sent was a pulled record image—flat, clinical, detached, a record a medical examiner released to the national missing person database. He looked like anybody's brother, somebody's father, someone's grown kid who should've been expected home by now. I stared at the image, longer than I meant to, the cold fluorescent light leaching all color from his skin.

A shudder crawled up my spine as I picture the unclaimed body at the morgue—skin waxen, eyes closed to secrets I'm not sure I want to know.

Great Perks. I pulled up their website: business travel and expense management, booking services for private lodging companies. Just a plain, empty site—no affiliates, no partners, no real footprint. A polished shell with nothing behind it.

No links, no obvious connections. No neat lines tying him to the others.

The name sits there on my screen, plain and unhelpful.

Maybe it's nothing. Maybe it's just a newer company—still small, still invisible in a crowded industry where staying quiet keeps bigger players from circling in to steal your contracts. Travel booking systems aren't flashy. They don't need to be. They live in the background, humming along while money moves through them.

Plenty of legitimate businesses look like that at first—no real online footprint, no public partnerships, no chatter. Just enough information to exist. Just enough to take clients who don't want attention either.

I scroll again, looking for something I've missed. A link. A name. Anything. There's nothing there. And maybe that's normal. Maybe I'm forcing connections that aren't real, stitching meaning into gaps because my brain doesn't know how to stop once it starts.

Or maybe this is exactly how something stays hidden.

Were these just dead men Jay happened to be researching—loose ends brushing the edges of the travel industry?

Or were they murdered, systematically, and Jay knew something he wasn't supposed to?

Arrrgh.

It feels like crawling under a table for a dozen missing puzzle pieces, trying to assemble the picture upside down. And if it's murder—what makes someone do it? What makes a person take a life and leave a soul floundering, untethered, desperate to escape its own body?

That question drifts through my head, tangled with a million others.

Did I pay the electric bill?

Why is the mortgage always scraped together in nickels and dimes, at the last gasp before payment's due?

What if Shane doesn't make the team?

He'll be devastated. I don't think he can take another loss.

Sometimes he looks at me like he's already mourning something—eyes hollowed, shoulders taut—before he slips the mask back on, smooth and practiced, hiding whatever's churning underneath. Or maybe he knows something I don't. Maybe that's the guilt I catch darting across his face before it disappears.

The thought hits me at three a.m.—sharp and cold as a slap. I'm wide awake as I ease upright in bed. I groan. My back hurts. My arm hurts. Tina Metzger used me as a punching bag on Saturday. I'd missed Thursday's class. She wasn't happy.

To make matters worse, I'd gotten a little cocky after sparring with the guy on Jay's stairway and pulling off that full-throttle, classic kick at the park. Tina is built like a wall— more muscle in her shoulders and arms than Elle, a ruddy complexion, vivid blue eyes that stand out against her dark buzz cut.

Once she straps on the boxing gloves, mouthguard, and headgear, she looks like a villain from a comic-book movie. I, on the other hand, with my hair frizzing out from under the helmet, look like a dancing clown in a comedy flick.

On Saturday, she feinted back once while correcting my form, putting on a show for the little kids' gym class clustered nearby, and launched into her usual taunt. "Boo, hoo, hoo—" she crooned, rubbing a glove against my shoulder.

For reasons I still can't explain, I decided to be cheeky. I pulled my arm back and clocked her square in the face.

"And boo, hoo, hoo back," I mimicked, throwing in a little swagger as she dropped onto her rear.

It was a bold move. Also, it was an incredibly stupid one.

Her eyes went wide—silver-dollar wide. That moment has replayed in my head for the last two nights. She popped back up, feinted once, then took off after me, and I spent the next thirty seconds sprinting laps around the gym with Tina in hot pursuit while a crowd of kids and their parents laughed themselves breathless.

Now it's just a bad memory I can't fix. And this week, Tina will make sure I don't forget it.

The house is so quiet I can hear the faint tick of the hallway clock and the low, steady hum of the heater breathing through the vents. Daisy is pressed against one side, Annie on the other. I must've fallen asleep reading to them in Daisy's room. They're warm and heavy with sleep, mouths curved in soft, unconscious smiles, tangled into me like they belong there.

I can't sleep. At least they can.

I smile. Their peace seeps into me, for a moment, like sunlight across a cold floor.

Ryder snaps into my mind—the way he jumped up from his desk when he saw me in his office doorway and spilled his coffee all over the paperwork. The memory makes me giggle quietly to myself. He's cute, I decide, maybe not carrying as much ego as he did in high school. It was nice to see a bit of a smile on his lips.

I shove back frizzy hair from my face and feel it slide down my shoulders and back, wild as ever. The echo of Ryder's yelp when the coffee hit his pants still rings in my ears, and I can almost smell the sharp tang of fresh coffee, hear the clatter of his mug on the desk, the way he laughed it off, cheeks flushed.

Oh. That must have been who Ricky was talking about when he said "my boyfriend." He was making a joke.

Carefully, I wiggle free, easing myself from between them. In the dim hallway, I pass the neat stack of folders for Wally tomorrow—files that feel heavier than paper has any right to be. The paper edges rasp against each other when I move them, a dry, papery whisper. There's a new scribble on the wall, bright orange and defiant—crayon shavings dust the floor beneath it. I should be annoyed, but all I can think is: at least someone in this house isn't afraid to leave a mark. I shuffle through Jay's files again. The paper edges bite at my fingertips—tiny stings, reminders that some answers draw blood. Beyond that, on the kitchen table, are the folders I took from Jay's house.

I stop there. Stare at them. What do they have to do with Jay? Is he dead—or alive?

I'd called the police station earlier and gotten permission to go back to the house. Forensics must be finished with Jay's disappearance by now. The place should be empty of answers.

But I know better. Paper remembers what people try to forget. Somewhere in those folders is the reason Jay vanished—or the reason someone wanted him to. I lay them out, again and again, waiting for answers to leap out at me. I scour the internet for any detail that ties it all together. Maybe I'm overthinking. Then I get nosy and look up folks just outside my circle. Beth Ann—her social feeds full of beach days and family reunions. Ricky, all basketball and soccer teams. And his wife, Eloise Darling—what? *Elle.*

Oh. That's why he asked me why I tried to get his wife killed. I barely caught it—he was talking nonstop as we dashed across a busy street. I thought I'd misheard him, too distracted by thoughts of the missing men and all the loose ends.

I asked, "Huh?" He glanced back and echoed, "Huh?"—then immediately launched into another ramble about basketball.

The name clicks into place, and I wonder why I never put two and two together before. The Darlings are practically a landmark around here—building houses, fixing roofs, patching foundations, wiring barns. If something breaks in Pinehaven, chances are a Darling's worked on it at least once. It's the kind of last name you grow up hearing without ever really seeing.

What surprises me isn't the business—it's Ricky.

Back in high school, Ricky Bradley dated half the cheerleading squad, most of the tennis team, and enough soccer girls to make it a running joke. Always the same type: pretty, agreeable, a little fluff-headed. The kind who laughed at his jokes and never asked uncomfortable questions.

So, I never expected him to marry someone with edges. Someone with grit—a woman who'd sweep a room with just her stare and dare you to challenge her.

I remember the way Elle used to stare me down across the volleyball net, jaw set, daring me to flinch first. Some people mellow with age. Elle just got sharper.

Then it clicks again—*Elle.* Volleyball team. Strong legs.

Loud laugh. Didn't take nonsense from anyone. I remember her now, not as a blur but as a spark—vague, yet bright enough to feel stupid for forgetting.

Maybe Ricky's deeper than I gave him credit for.

Or maybe people just grow up in ways you don't notice— until it matters.

I blink and scroll back, suddenly more interested than I should be. I'm nosy, and it's three in the morning, and my brain has decided this is productive.

She owns Do-It-All Darling Contracting. I picture her in coveralls, hair pulled back, boots muddy and grin sharp as a box cutter.

Huh.

I sit back, staring at the screen, the laptop's glow washing the kitchen in pale light. My mind rearranges pieces without asking permission.

The memory of Jay's empty house creeps in—the echo of a door creaking just after I'd sworn I was alone. The sound still sends goosebumps up my arms.

I wonder if she could take a look at Jay's house—see if anyone messed with the back door to get in.

Or if whoever broke in that night didn't need to. Maybe they already had a key.

Chapter —20

"When were you planning to tell me you're married to Ricky?" I ask two days later, peering over Elle's broad shoulder as she runs her hand along Jay's doorframe, checking for splinters, scratches—anything that might say forced entry. "I didn't know until yesterday," I add. "Ricky asked me—out of nowhere—why I was trying to get you killed at Winslow Park."

I'm not short or spindly, but beside her I feel like a compact Honda wedged next to a Mack truck. She blocks out the foyer light, her presence a wall of muscle and purpose. That finally gets her attention—not her face, just the pause. Her hand stills on the frame.

Then her face tightens. "Wait. Why?" she asks, still facing the door. "Were you looking to date Ricky?" Without warning, she breaks into a high-knee jog in place—arms pumping, knees snapping up. Her calves flex like braided cables. She could probably bench-press me and the doorframe both. I remind myself, again, never to get on her bad side. "Is that why you thought he was running with you?"

"No, I—"

She's just as assertive now as she was bouncing dodgeballs off my head in school. I wonder how she and Ricky manage at home. Their marriage must be thunder and lightning—loud, spectacular, probably destructive to nearby furniture. His approach this morning, when I cautiously eased the topic into conversation, had been: *Is this why you're running with me— to get a discount toilet leak fixed?*

"Ohhh, I get it." Her lip twitches. She gives me a knowing nod. "You're wondering why ol' lady-killer Ricky Bradley would settle down with someone like me? No, he did not get me pregnant."

"For heaven's sake—no," I say. "I was just wondering why *he* isn't taking your kids to school since he heads that way anyway. You barreled through the school zone this morning like you were gunning for Daytona—nearly clipped my bumper."

"Oh, I had a leaky faucet on Main I had to fix." She thumbs over her shoulder. "That was you? I slowed right at the twenty-mile-an-hour sign."

"No, no, Elle. You absolutely did not. You came up on my rear end and tried to pass me. I had to brace for impact."

"I thought I heard screaming," she says thoughtfully. "That was you?"

"Elle, it was everybody in my car *and* three cars in front of me. Even Shane hit soprano."

She lets out a smoky laugh, and I instinctively tense, bracing for an elbow. She's already nailed me twice—hard, right in the ribs. I'll be wearing the bruise for days.

"But it's football season," she says. "If you want to go lock yourself into the announcer's booth and pull a *Baby Come Back*, I can make it happen—but he probably won't budge, because I've already got my big boy handled."

Baby Come Back. Ugh.

He must relay our running conversations to her.

It's strange running into people from high school, because the only thing linking you anymore is that shared knot of memories from back then. So when you talk, you end up fishing for the same old stories—the ones you both remember—just to get the conversation moving.

With Ricky and me on our first couple of runs, it started with Bobby Peterson.

Bobby was drama club and theater—lead roles, every time. He was good. Really good. He was also all ego, which made him unbearable. He'd walk down the hallways and suddenly burst into song, something we all found unsettling back then, even if we didn't have the language for why.

Chrissy Adams—the cheerleader—thought he was destined to be a movie star. And to be fair, he wasn't ugly. He just wasn't average—he had that news anchor look: upturned nose, chiseled yet somehow bland features.

They dated through junior and senior year. Then Chrissy fell for some other guy and left Bobby wrecked enough that, during a football game, he locked himself in the announcer's booth and grabbed the microphone.

He didn't sing a real song. He just made it up as he went—off-key, looping the same desperate lines about second chances and promises he couldn't keep—until the cops had to break the door open.

After that, *Baby Come Back* became shorthand for the ultimate public humiliation—what happens when someone wants a person too badly and everyone else gets a front-row seat.

"I'll pass," I say. "He's all yours."

She straightens, pokes a thick finger at the doorframe. "Whoever came in didn't force entry. I checked every door and window. Only one was open—the one you said you jimmied. It's locked now."

Her voice drops, more serious than I've seen it yet.

She glances at Beth Ann, who's scooping papers into a garbage bag with quick, practiced swipes. "So, you invite me out here to give Shane a leg up?"

"Huh?"

"You know," she says, nodding toward Beth Ann. "Did you bring your—what does she call it—your Broke Moms Detective Club together so Ricky puts Shane on the team?"

"Well, it isn't actually a club," I mutter, shooting Beth Ann a look. She just shrugs. "And... is that something people do?"

Apparently, yes.

I sigh. "No, strategic planning is not my strong suit. If I'd thought ahead, I would have cornered the band director for a backroom deal or at least begged for a coupon before buying Molly's trumpet."

"Oh, you went with rent-to-own, didn't you?" she says, nodding with the solemn pity of someone who's seen too many school fundraisers.

"Guilty as charged. But for Jay's door, I just needed someone who wouldn't ask too many questions." I pause, then add, "And if we're swapping secrets, fair warning—I pay in gratitude and leftover Halloween candy."

"It just looked fun," Elle says. "She sent pictures of you all at your so-called pizza party."

"It wasn't a party," I say. "It was frozen pizza. Paper plates." I tilt my head. "And ice cream."

"Don't worry about it." Her jaw tightens anyway, and she

brushes past me, heading for the door. "I know when I'm not wanted." She nods—too casual, too practiced—trying to shrug off what's sitting heavy between us. "This isn't high school anymore. We've all grown up, right?"

I do. But I also know she's mentally sizing me up, like she's got that stinking old rubber dodgeball cocked and ready. She played so much, her body just knows what to do—no thought required, just instinct. She never missed. I find myself squinting, instinctively turning my head, bracing for the hit.

She pauses, lets out a sharp breath. "But after what happened at Winslow Park—after the guy never got caught—Ricky kept running with you because he was worried. That guy could still be out there. Lurking somewhere. Watching women who run alone."

There it is. Bam. Right between the eyes.

She lets out a grunt—half-laugh, half-surrender. "And honestly? I think you've actually grown on him."

I blink. Did she really go for a second throw while I was still reeling from the first?

"You and your ridiculous habit of jumping into every puddle just to splash him—like a two-year-old," she adds, rolling her eyes. "If I'd known math geeks were this competitive in high school, I would've stuck you on the volleyball team. Ricky's lost three pounds trying to keep up."

Beth Ann shoots me daggers and jabs a finger toward Elle's back.

What? I mouth.

Let her in the club, she mouths back.

"There is no club—" I groan (internally and out loud this

time) and dart forward, blocking the door before Elle can step out.

I stick out my hand. "Okay. Fine. Welcome to the... um... Broke Moms Detective Agency. Club." I wince. "We can't really call it that. I've got my license, but Wally would murder me if he knew I was moonlighting. This is all extremely unofficial. Technically undercover. Except not really—"

Elle turns back, half-smiling now, and shakes my hand.

"Three Broke Moms Detective Agency," she says.

And just like that, the club exists. "Okay, come on and I'll show you something secret to make it official."

Jay has a hidey-hole I only know about. He probably doesn't even realize I caught him using it—except that night I pretended to sleep on the couch and watched him slip something inside. I doubt he'd want Beth Ann or Elle to know, but considering it was an engagement ring—and that he left with the kids not long after—I give three rounds of cheers to an old book called *Euphues*, which taught, if nothing else, that love and war have never followed the rules of fair play.

"So maybe a month before he left, he put an engagement ring in here." I turn, give them both a glare and an outstretched hand before they ask. I didn't bring the other thing—the basket, the names—because once you let that out, you can't put it back. "And don't ask how I know. You'd both be curious too if you caught your boyfriend slinking around and hiding things."

"Oh no," Beth Ann hisses. "That's like—horrible."

"Um. I wasn't making wedding plans, if that's what you

think. But it made for some sleepless nights, wondering what I'd do if he asked me."

Elle stares at me, unconvinced.

"Okay, maybe I flipped through a few wedding magazines in the checkout line," I sigh. I crouch, sliding aside a stack of old coats. My fingers brush dust and cedar shavings. There's a tiny door with a tarnished knob behind the shelving. I tug it open, heart stuttering. "Bingo," I say—too brightly.

Elle leans in over my shoulder. "You look like someone who just found buried treasure."

"Yeah," Beth Ann says, popping her wintergreen gum—pop, pop. "With Misty, that's usually a corpse."

"Haha," I say flatly, rolling my eyes. Then I shrug. "You're probably right." I swipe on my phone's flashlight and peer inside. Oh. The ring is still there. Velvet box, corners scuffed and battered, as though someone opened and closed it a dozen times, hesitating at the threshold. My throat constricts, my body remembering long before my brain catches up.

Beth Ann sucks in a breath. "Is that—"

"Yeah," I say. "That's the one he was hiding."

Elle goes quiet, which for her is alarming. She shifts her weight, muscles tensing, eyes scanning the room like it might suddenly turn hostile. "And that?" she asks.

Beside the ring, wrapped in a faded dish towel, sits a compact pistol. Not flashy. Not oversized. Just... deliberate. Beth Ann's gum freezes mid-pop. "Did he have a gun before?" she whispers.

"No," I answer. "He didn't." I reach deeper, fingertips brushing something smooth and rectangular beneath the towel. I pull it free—a phone. Not Jay's. Too clean, too blank. No case, no scratches, powered off, SIM slot empty.

Beth Ann's gum pops once. Then stops. "Ten bucks says that's a burner," she says quietly. "You know, the ones you can buy along with a $50 gift card, and it can't be traced."

Elle and I look at her cautiously.

"Don't look at me like that. People come in and buy them all the time at the dollar store," she quickly adds. "Well, the ones who you'd suspect. Like Eddy Thompson and Jeanie Littleton who deal drugs."

Elle straightens. "I doubt he'd leave that behind if he knew he was leaving."

"No," I say, staring at it. "That screams, 'I'm being watched.'" The air thickens. The walls lean in, listening.

Beth Ann swallows. "So... what happened? Why'd you break up with him?"

"I didn't." The words come out flat. I glance at them both, then back into the hidey-hole. There is a little scratch pad of paper not much bigger than my hand. I pull it out. The curled papers had peeled away from the pad, but held together by a single paperclip. "We were sitting at the table one night. Me, him, the kids. He says, 'Guess what, kids—we're moving to California.'"

Elle's eyebrows shoot up. I ruffle the pages of the papers, narrow my eyes to fine slits. It is just a few pages, Jay's hard to read scribbles all over it. There's a card attached with a staple for the Pinehaven Historical Society. "And you said...?"

"I wasn't invited," I say. "A week later, they were gone."

"Just like that?" Beth Ann asks.

"Just like that," I repeat. "Three years." I shrug. "After a few days of sobbing, I realized I was more attached to the kids than him. He wasn't home much. I think I was more a nanny than a girlfriend."

Elle lets out a low whistle between her teeth. "That's cold."

"And this?" Beth Ann gestures toward the gun, the phone, the ring. "This doesn't feel like someone who just... left."

"No," I say again. "It feels like someone who planned to come back." Silence settles in, thick and uneasy.

Elle exhales slowly. "Okay. Let's say someone wanted him quiet. Or gone. Or scared enough to disappear."

Beth Ann nods. "And let's say they figured the fastest way to flush him out would be through the kids."

My stomach drops.

"Or through you," Elle adds.

I close the little door gently, like if I'm careful enough, everything might behave itself again. I still hold the pad of paper.

"We don't tell a soul about this," I say. "Not yet."

Beth Ann nods immediately. Elle hesitates—then rolls her eyes and bobs her head once in reluctant agreement.

"What's that?" Elle asks, pointing at the papers in my hand. I didn't know. I can't decipher much. It just looks like scribbles and doodles, a bunch of little tornadoes sketched over and over.

When Jay was nervous, he always reached for the closest thing to doodle on—a napkin, a used envelope, paper. Smiley faces, Xs, little ghosts. He'd doodle away. But the tornadoes meant he was getting panicky.

The curled edges meant his thumb was scrubbing them over and over. When he was in full edgy mode, every corner was bent and wrinkled. Just like these notes. Something was definitely wrong.

I shrug. They don't need to know everything. I just poke at the business card. "He must have been digging for something historical," I mutter. "Who knows. Jay is an enigma." Or was.

I rest my forehead against the shelf, breathing in dust, stale wool, and something sour—regret prickling at the back of my tongue. My voice comes out thin. "I'm sorry to drag you into this." The words scrape my throat. "And I'd go straight to the police—if I knew they weren't mixed up in it. But whoever ran into me that night sneaking around could have been a cop. "

I straighten and hold up the front door key so they can see it. "This is the only key Shane had. I checked everywhere they could've hidden another. The police had access to the house. Someone there could've gone through Jay's things."

Maybe that lands. Maybe it doesn't. But the truth has already settled in my chest, a lump of lead pressing down on every breath.

As much as I want to believe Jay took the kids to keep them safe, the evidence screams otherwise. They were never his priority. Work always came first.

Shane mentioned once—offhand, like it slipped out—that they were always on the move in California, bouncing from cash-only hotels to threadbare highway motels that reeked of mildew and old smoke.

The kids missed school, living out of suitcases, their lives packed and unpacked in a new place every week. Dragging them along wasn't protection. It was inconvenience.

Or worse—a human shield against whoever was chasing them.

A shiver snakes down my spine as I picture Daisy, her small hand in Jay's, skipping past a broken neon sign at some grimy roadside inn—her freckled face upturned to him, beaming. And somewhere, high above, a sniper sighting down at them through dirty glass. The thought curdles in my gut, bitter and cold as old coffee left out all night.

Jay didn't disappear to save them.

He disappeared because he could save himself.

Taking the kids slowed him down. Leaving them behind didn't.

Somewhere along the way, running became the plan—and whether he meant to or not, he made me an unwilling accomplice. The shame of it burns in my gut, hot and relentless. Maybe he didn't have time to warn me. Or maybe he just didn't care to. Signing those guardianship papers is the only proof I have that he knew something bad was coming.

Whatever Jay was running from, he left me behind to sweep up the wreckage—shards of trust piercing deeper every day. And to protect the kids—because he wouldn't. My hands curl tight, knuckles white, as if I could squeeze the fear right out of me.

Chapter −21

I drop Wally's folders on his desk just before lunch. No lingering. No commentary. He flips through them with the same bored efficiency he applies to everything that matters, then stills—just a fraction too long. "Careful," he says, not looking up. "You're starting to ask questions that don't belong to you."

The fluorescent light above drones, bathing the room in jaundiced yellow. My skin tingles, as if someone's thumb sinks into the back of my neck—a tingling of scrutiny, even with Wally's gaze glued to the file. The air stinks of scorched coffee and brittle paper, a scent buried in every crevice of his office, pungent as a warning.

My stomach knots. "About what?"

He finally meets my eyes. "Missing persons. Case files no one touches. Regional. Somebody noticed."

Not because I'd been loud—because I'd been consistent.

I frown. I haven't talked to anyone. Not officially. Not off the record. I haven't even pushed yet—just looked, quietly, the way I always do. "Who?" My voice comes out a little too sharp. A little too curious.

He closes the folder. "Doesn't matter."

"It does if you're warning me."

He sighs, irritation roughening his voice. "I'm not telling you who said it. I'm telling you to stop before you make yourself memorable."

"Memorable?" I echo, stretching the word into a dare. "What does that mean?" I study his face, hunting for that twitch in his jaw—his old tell. I wave my hands with exaggerated flair, rolling my shoulders in a mock swagger. "I'm already extraordinary and unforgettable. Look at this— that's why you hired me. Well, and my remarkable brain."

Wally's mouth twitches, half amused, half annoyed.

"No, I hired you to blend in. Be inconspicuous, ordinary." He clears his throat. "I hired you to sit in cars and watch. Take photos. Go to restaurants and look like any woman ordering a meal—just watching, just observing, nothing else. You do the grunt work. I handle the data, the planning, the delegation. Crime-solving is for the cops—we investigate. If you can't stick to those guidelines, there are a hundred other women with frizzy ginger hair and too many freckles who would fit the bill better. And without that short-tempered attitude. Are you still listening to the tapes?"

"Yes." That's enough. Ego cracked. "And I do have a lot of freckles," I muster. Wally doesn't bluff, but he doesn't invent problems either. He'd drop me in a heartbeat. It doesn't take much to trail someone without being seen. But this is different. Someone talked—someone close enough to notice.

"I didn't go around asking anyone for information, if that's what you're implying," I say. "It just lands in my lap before I even walk in the room."

"That's what worries me," he replies.

He slides a photo across the desk—a girl, maybe fifteen, blonde hair, blue eyes, chin tilted like she's daring the world to try her. A slip of paper follows, addresses scrawled in a hurried, nearly illegible hand.

Wally lowers his voice. "Police called her a runaway. Case

went cold last year. Her parents got a call—a tip that someone saw her. She goes by Deedee. Stick to the rules. Just need to know if she's alive, and where she's being seen."

He doesn't meet my eyes as he files away the folders, but his tone is unyielding. The case is mine—the rules are his.

He was giving me something else to hold—so I'd stop gripping Jay's disappearance.

But for my own job security, I need to wrap this up with something a little brighter.

"On a lighter note," I say, biting my lip as I start to turn. "You don't happen to have any of those affirmation tapes—'I choose peace,' 'I welcome serenity,' that sort of thing? Because I've got a kid learning trumpet, and my nervous system is filing a complaint."

"Go on, get out of here," he grunts. But the tension doesn't budge when I do—it clings, stubborn as dried glue, and follows me out the door. That part belongs to me alone.

~

Shane's tryout drags on. The gym is a soup of sweat and rubber soles, the shrill whistle snapping through the air and scraping my nerves raw. When Coach Bradley finally calls him over, Shane's face is pinched, guarded—already bracing for disappointment.

Coach claps a heavy hand on his shoulder. "You've got potential," he says. "Good instincts. But you're raw. You make the team—but you're going to work. A lot."

Shane blinks. "I-I made it?" His voice comes out small, tentative, thin as thread.

Coach nods. "If you want to keep it."

Shane glances at me, searching my face to see if this is real. I nod, lips twitching. His grin flashes—quick, bright, like something alive broke loose in his chest. Then I see his eyes stray toward the door to the gym. A form wavers there, just outside the threshold. Noah Ryder. I see him nod at Shane, a slight smile parting his lips. Shane nods back and Ryder disappears. He made it look like he'd been there for something mundane—forms, keys, a signature—but knowing this small town, he'd come for a reason: just to make sure Shane got there okay, and to let him see, without saying it out loud, that somebody was in his corner.

On the drive home, Shane is quiet, staring out the window. A half-smile ghosts his lips—already plotting how hard he'll push himself. I should feel lighter, but Wally's warning lingers, prickling and cold. Someone noticed me. I can't remember giving anyone a reason to notice at all.

The town blurs by under sodium lights and rain-streaked glass. Something sharp coils at my spine—a warning, or a new mess. I grip the wheel tighter, knuckles white.

"I hope Coach didn't pick me for the team because he's scared of you," Shane says, glancing over with a grin he's trying very hard to suppress.

"What?" I ask. "Why would you think that?"

He bites his lip, fails. "The teachers take turns standing outside in the mornings. I guess he heard you... yelling your tapes."

"I was *affirming*," I say.

Shane snorts.

"Oh," I say, staring straight ahead. Then I turn, cross my

eyes at him, and face the road again.

The joke lands. The moment passes. But the worry doesn't.

I don't know if the kids are safe. I know Wally has his own best interests in mind—he always has. Still, sometimes you do what you have to do to protect your people.

And right now, we aren't.

Tomorrow, I'll start the job.

Find Deedee.

Find whoever's watching me.

Tonight, the darkness feels close—thick, restless, lurking. My phone vibrates once on the nightstand. Unknown number. No message. I stare, nerves sparking, and listen to the rain. For a second, a shadow stirs outside the window—a trick of the streetlights, or not.

Deedee is out there somewhere, a missing girl with a trail gone cold. But someone else is circling me—someone who knows I've started looking in places I shouldn't. Two mysteries. Two separate shadows. And the feeling, crawling down my spine, that one is about to find me before I find the other.

Outside, rain ticks against the glass. Somewhere, a siren wails, threading danger through the quiet. In a small town, sounds like this always bring worry—everyone knows everyone. Is it ninety-one-year-old Mrs. Grant, alone with her army of cats? Or did one of the kids skateboarding under the damp streetlights after dark take a spill and break an arm? I let the darkness settle and wait for morning.

Chapter –22

Noah Ryder shows up on my porch just after dinner, a plastic clamshell of store-bought cookies tucked under his arm like evidence. Chocolate chip. Generic brand. A dollar-store Christmas bow taped on top—no card, no explanation, just Ryder logic. He gives me a crooked smile, as if this is a perfectly normal thing for a grown man to do on a Tuesday night in Pinehaven.

"Heard Shane made the team," he says. "Figured that deserved sugar. Grocery was closed and the dollar store freezers were out, so this was the next best thing."

He glances past me, where Shane's laughter bounces off the wallpaper for the first time in days. Ryder's mouth twitches— not quite a smile, but close. "Didn't want to make a big thing," he adds, shoving the cookies at me like they might detonate.

Beth Ann had texted me earlier from behind the register. Ryder, apparently, had been haunting the store for an hour and a half with one of those little red hand baskets looped over his arm. He'd pick something up, then put it back. Chips. Cookies. A box of mildly thawed miniature chocolate éclairs. At one point, Beth Ann followed a trail of popsicle juice with a mop and discovered he'd broken into the freezer, ripped off the tape barring the ice cream case, and peeled back the barrier to haul out three partially melted boxes like a man on a mission. She made him dump them straight into the garbage.

I didn't let on that I already knew about his reckless adventure at Pinehaven Discount Dollar. What shocked me most was realizing we were the reason he'd gone down that particular path.

"We're eating spaghetti tonight," I mumble, glancing at the dining room where Molly is one second from screaming, "Food fight!" Daisy and Annie are already catapulting meatballs at each other.

I imagine it can't be easy for him to come here, given our awkward past. Still, Mom and Dad never turned anyone away who showed up at the door during a meal. It usually meant they were lonely or hungry. With five brothers, it always meant open access to the fridge and a place at the table.

"Come on in," I say. "We just sat down."

And, by some small miracle, he does. Of course he does. Ryder—king of questionable timing and dollar-store cookies— shrugs like it's nothing and wipes his shoes on the mat like he's done it a hundred times before.

"That was amazing," he tells me later, drying plates. "Thanks." He barely spoke during dinner—I figured kids made him nervous. I was wrong. About halfway through the meal, I got up to grab more Parmesan. I'm pretty sure Daisy launched a meatball at Molly, because I caught Ryder's hand shoot up out of the corner of my eye and heard a wet smack. A second later—while I was elbow-deep in the fridge—there was a muffled burst of cheering, the quiet kind that means something went right.

When I came back, everyone had gone suspiciously still, mouths pressed flat, trying not to burst out laughing, eyes shining. Ryder was clearly attempting to hide the meatball in his fist, then discreetly pass it to Nacho under the table to get rid of the evidence. I found it later, untouched, tucked beside his chair—evidence neither he nor Daisy's fat cat had quite figured out what to do with.

It's usually Shane and Molly's turn for dishes, but tonight I worried it might look like child labor. They sprint to the living room to claim the TV. Molly and Shane have a new tradition: launching themselves over the couch armrests and landing with a bounce on either end. Daisy and Annie burrow into the toy box, flinging toys to see who can reach the bottom first.

"It was dollar-store spaghetti sauce," I admit, "with red pepper, ketchup, and brown sugar. Honestly, it was worth having you over just to see how well-behaved they were. I was positive Molly was about to start an all-out meatball war, but the second they saw you, they practically held hands and sang kumbaya."

"They don't think I'm here to spy on them, do they?"

"Are you?"

"No." He looks at me, then quickly away. For the first time, I realize I'm tilting my head up—he's taller than I remember, which is saying something, since I usually know everyone in town by the top of their hair.

"I'm just trying to make sure they know I'm not a monster," he says quietly. "That what the police and agencies are doing isn't about ripping them away from the only thing that's been consistent for them." He hesitates. "Which is you."

When I look up, he's wearing a lopsided half-smile, like he's holding back a laugh. "And I wanted to make sure you could outrun ol' Metzger. Didn't want to go looking for you and find you dead behind the community building dumpster."

Oh. No.

My head jerks up, cheeks flaming. With my pale, freckled skin, embarrassment flashes neon. "You saw that?"

"We had a county-wide CPR class." He finds this so funny he starts laughing—an honest-to-God guffaw that echoes down the hall. The kids peek into the kitchen, eyes wide, like something exploded in the oven.

"Fantastic," I mutter as he doubles over. "Glad to be your comic relief."

"I'm sorry—I'm so—" He tries to stop, but it takes a solid five minutes. By then, the kids had wandered in, and of course, Daisy and Annie had already seen it happen. At one point, I hid behind Annie, knowing Tina wouldn't hit a child. Shane and Molly had been in the other room shooting baskets.

Now everyone's in on it.

The rest of the night turns into a kids' movie, Ryder's cookies, and the last of the milk I'd planned to save for cereal. We even try the armrest leap like the kids and end up smacking heads. Another bruise to add to the collection— courtesy of Tina and my own ego.

At bedtime, I walk Ryder to the door—me taking two steps onto the porch, him one step down. "Heard you're running with Ricky," he says. Small talk. Reaching for familiar ground.

"Yeah. He talks football, basketball, strange protein shakes, and when conversation stalls—Bobby Peterson."

"I heard. He uses the community center gym around the same time I do." There's a pause, then, "Bobby's married to some supermodel now. Runs a theater company in New York."

"Well," I say, "I'm glad I managed to feed you and humiliate myself in one evening."

He smiles then—not big, not showy—just a quick flash of something warm in his eyes, like he's caught the joke and knows better than to say it out loud. He turns. "Maybe you'd want to go out sometime?"

My head snaps up. "Go out. Like a date?" I immediately want to sink into the porch boards.

"Yeah."

I'm staring too hard. Mouth probably open. Guys like Noah Ryder don't ask women like me out. They go for women with no backstory, no baggage, no kids tugging at their sleeves. And of course, that's the exact moment Molly unleashes her first note on the trumpet—a sound so piercing it makes the windows tremble and Ryder jump a solid inch sideways. We both chuckle, low and conspiratorial, like we're in on the joke together.

"I don't know," I say. "I've got…" I gesture at the house. "Trumpet payments until I'm eighty. Bills. Laundry. Kids. Work. I'm digging quarters out of the couch for lunch money and gas. It's just not a good time." I let out a breathless laugh. "But I appreciate it."

I stick out my hand like a total idiot.

He looks at it like I suddenly sprouted horns, but shakes it anyway.

"If it was the spaghetti," I blurt, "I can give you the recipe."

"Sure," he says, still baffled, and disappears into the darkness, leaving the porch creaking and the air thick with questions.

Chapter −23

I wasn't looking for answers. I was just killing time.

Now I'm running barefoot down a cold, unforgiving beach, my heels sinking and slipping in the sand. The wind shoves me sideways, sharp grains biting at my cheeks and lips. The sky isn't hinting at a storm—it's barreling straight at us, bruised and heavy, thunder vibrating in my bones.

Us.

"Run!" I shout, clinging to the girl's hand behind me. "You've got to go faster!"

She's gulping air. I'm gulping air. In the back of my mind, I'm cursing out Wally. A raise. I am definitely asking for a raise. Getting chased by a stranger with a gun goes well beyond my job description—sitting in cars, watching, observing. Nothing dangerous. Not this.

Earlier—before any of this mattered. Wally had planted me on the beach with a long lens and a bad angle, waiting for a girl who might show or might already be gone. The beach was empty.

Cold. The sun was high enough to bleach the water flat— the kind of afternoon where nothing dramatic ever happens and you invent errands just to feel useful.

I shifted in the sand, and checked my watch. Then checked it again, like it might change its mind.

I pulled the folder onto my lap.

It wasn't thick. That bothered me.

Thick folders meant messes—loud ones. This was neat. Names. Dates. A few clipped forms. Paperwork that looked harmless until you noticed how often it repeated.

John Garcia.

I kept coming back to him. Maybe it was the morgue photo Beth Ann had sent from the database. It made Jay feel dead too, and my chest ached with it. Molly had leaned in my doorway the night before, like she always does, asking if I'd heard anything about her dad. If I'd found out something new.

I'd told her no. Later, I sat on the edge of her bed for two hours, rubbing her back, running my fingers through her hair while she cried herself to sleep.

"I missed you doing this, like when I was little," she whispered. "Especially when Dad left us at those hotels for days. I'd imagine you doing this. We never knew if he'd come back. Every knock on the door freaked us out. We thought it was the hotel guy, or the cops coming to kick us out because nobody paid. Or maybe they knew we were alone. It was scary."

My failure to solve her dad's disappearance bit deep—like a car door slamming on bare fingers. I wanted to say something to make it better, but the words stuck, useless, behind my teeth. So, I kept searching, fixated on John Garcia, convinced he was the key to everything. Because now, I'd hit a dead end with Jay—there was nothing new left to find.

On paper, John's name sat exactly where it always had. Not at the top. Not buried. Just there. Taxes. Bookkeeping. Compliance. The boring things everyone hands off and forgets.

John hadn't owned anything. He hadn't managed anything. He'd just kept it straight.

Beth Ann finding him on NamUs had felt random at the time. Wrong place. Wrong day. But his name didn't feel random here. It felt central. Like a hinge you don't notice until the door comes off.

I closed the folder and stared out at the water, letting the thought settle. Push too hard, and you start convincing yourself of things that aren't there—I'd learned that the hard way.

I had tried ten times to call the Pinehaven Historical Society to see why Jay might have visited there, might have their card. I just get a message saying they're closed most of the winter due to volunteer staffing. I am wracking my brain trying to think of anything of local historical value that would play into his game.

Nobody answers.

But Jay's tornados over and over on those notes just scream some kind of warning. With that thought in mind, I text Elle and Beth Ann a picture of a cat running into a wall trying to catch a mouse: *I feel like I am running into nothing but walls today. Know anybody who works for the historical society? I think they're all dead—*

My phone buzzed. I didn't answer right away. A family a few yards down wrestled with a striped umbrella, the wind snapping it inside out. Someone laughed. Someone swore. Life, loud and messy and unrelated.

Then I answered.

By the third call, a pattern started to hum—not loud enough to name. Same company mentioned twice. Same shrug when I asked who handled the filings.

"Oh, that stuff? John did," the woman said. "I think they called it the Foundation. Not officially—just what we called it. How's he doing, by the way? I heard he went abroad. He was great at grants. We met through Great Perks. They run our reservation system."

"Are you a nonprofit?"

"Yes. Mt. Olive Visitors Bureau. If you see him, tell him hi."

I wasn't telling her that I couldn't.

When the girl still didn't show, I opened my browser and typed in the names—Mt. Olive Visitors Bureau. Great Perks. The phone asked if I wanted to use location services. Sure, why not. As soon as I said yes, it pulled up local events and news—right there at the top, a report about a drowning.

Curiously, I clicked on the report. The newspaper photo loaded.

The pier.

I blinked. Looked up. *Same place.* Right here.

Another drowning. Morgan Hughes—three months earlier. The swimming accident they didn't question.

The same place as John Garcia. I knew he drowned.

I did not know it was here.

One pier. One stretch of beach. Two drownings—both victims with names from the folders I found at Jay's house. And me, right in the middle of it all.

Morgan Hughes showed up because of a memorial. His family had posted it online—candles, folded lawn chairs, a photo of them standing together at the end of the pier where he'd last been seen. It hadn't been there before. That was new.

Grief and phone location had pulled him back into the light.

I sat there, the folder warm against my knees, the ocean doing what it always does—covering its tracks, pretending it hadn't noticed a thing. Whatever this was, it wasn't screaming down a busy street. It was whispering in an empty alley. John Garcia had been right in the middle of it.

A knock on my window nearly sent me into the steering wheel. I've been jumpy since Winslow Park.

The woman stood there, early twenties, hair blown wild. Not the girl I was waiting for—but she was looking over her shoulder, panicked. Her palms smacked the glass. She grabbed the handle, yanking.

Locked. She spun, screamed—mouth wide open—and bolted around the back of the car.

Another shape stepped into view. Close—too close. Something black glinted over the hood. A gun.

Kids make you fast in ways nothing else does. You learn that when one reaches for a lit candle or bolts naked out the front door. But none of that prepares you for unlatching your seatbelt, throwing your door open, and slamming it into a man hard enough to send him staggering sideways.

I moved without thinking. Legs bent. Momentum carrying me through a half-crouch before I hit the sand.

The smart move would've been letting her in. But she'd already run.

I scrambled across the seat, shoved the door shut, locked it, and took off after her—doing everything Wally tells me not to do.

Barefoot, I was fast. Running with Ricky had made sure of that.

I caught her in under two minutes, grabbed her hand, and dragged her toward the hidden side of a crowded restaurant. Whoever had been chasing us slowed, then stopped, turning back toward the beach.

"What is going on?" I gasped, hands on my knees.

"Johnny didn't die here," she said. "He was murdered. In his apartment. I was there. Hiding. Nobody knows I said anything. Nobody—"

"He obviously knows something," I said, nodding toward the lone figure standing on the beach like a tourist.

"No. He just doesn't want me involved."

"Enough to kill us?"

"He's trying to protect us. Stop me from telling anybody," she whispered. "If they find out what we know, they'll kill us too. You need to go. Tell Ed my fees should be paid in full. I'm done bartering with him, being his stupid little informant."

Ed. Wally.

I stood there shaking as she slipped between two buildings, leaving me alone to make my way back to the car.

When I looked back toward the beach, the man with the gun was gone. Just footprints in the sand, already fading.

The beach looked empty again, like it had been all along. But now, every shadow felt like it was waiting. The storm was rolling in, the air heavy with the promise that all hell could break loose any moment.

Chapter −24

"Are you purposely trying to get me killed, or are you just rehearsing for some grand finale? Because I'm starting to see a pattern here, Wally." My voice is tight, anger simmering just beneath the surface. The storm pelts my windshield as I steer onto the muddy shoulder, wipers thrashing, ten miles from the coast. "First Winslow Park. Now the beach."

"What are you talking about?"

"You know exactly what I mean. You sent me to Myrtle Beach, where two guys connected to my ex were found dead— real suspicious, if you ask me. Drowned. And there was a source who knew exactly where I'd park."

"Oh. Huh?" I hear the crackle of paper—maybe he's stalling, maybe not. He clears his throat. "Oh—yeah. Where were you?"

"The beach. The pier."

"Oh no, I sent you to get a picture of the runaway— Deedee. At a restaurant. What would she be doing at the beach this time of year?"

"My question exactly. But that's where the address on your note led me, so that's where I went." I roll his Post-it note between my fingers, the ink smudged and damp from the storm. "The address on your note was exactly where I parked. While I was there, a girl—one of your sources—ran up to me, chased by a guy with a gun. She's done working for you. So obviously, Wally, you knew what you were doing."

"No, I specifically sent you to—oh." He stalls. "That explains why my witness never showed at the dive off the highway. Two Post-its. Same handwriting. Same ink. Stuck together like one note. Did you get what I needed?"

I assume his witness is the woman in the parking lot. "Why are you digging into Jay, Wally?" My voice drops. He has to know Jay was my ex by now. He has to know I have the kids. "Who's paying you to look into him? And why?"

Thunder cracks so loud it rattles the windshield, vibrating through my chest. The line goes dead-silent—long enough that I check my screen to make sure we're still connected.

"That is none of your concern," he says finally. "And even if I could, I can't divulge client information. What concern is it to you?"

"You know," I say. "I know you know. And it's my concern because to keep her from getting shot, I had to haul her toward the boardwalk restaurants—right out in the open. Jay is my ex-boyfriend. I'm the guardian of his kids. You're too sharp not to know that. And too careful to give me the wrong Post-it by accident." And a whole bunch of people seem to be dying around him. I don't say that. I clamp my mouth closed.

Silence.

"I can't share anything else," he says. "However—get over to the restaurant and see if Deedee is working. How far are you from the beach? I need a photo. And there's a car picking you up at eight tonight for surveillance at another restaurant. Free dinner. On me."

"I'm half an hour away and it's pouring," I say. "And you know I can't work nights last minute. I can't get a babysitter this late."

"Misty. When I hired you, you said you'd do anything for a

job. Nights. Weekends. I don't ask often. But if you can't handle it, you can always be—"

"Replaced."

I know.

In my town, jobs only exist at the school or city hall—and those come with a heaping side of nepotism. If you didn't play ball together in high school, you don't get hired.

"I get it," I say. "I need both addresses." I'm already counting backward—three hours and fifteen minutes until the school and bus run. And I still need a sitter.

Dress nice, Wally says. Like you're going on a date with someone who has good taste. Then he asks if I'm still driving that piece-of-crap soccer-mom SUV.

I tell him yes.

He groans like I've personally ruined his day and says he'll get a car—because appearances matter—but not without reminding me it's last minute, as if that inconvenience is somehow my fault.

"Then maybe pay me more," I mumble, more to myself than him.

He hears it. I know he does. I hear him grumble something about everyone having to make sacrifices to be a team player.

So somewhere in there I have to raid a thrift store for something that doesn't scream "mom"—or at least "mom on a budget." He wants single. No kids. Comfortable sitting alone at a table and owning it.

That pretty much sums up my life, minus the no-kids part. And the owning anything part.

I'm not above begging.

Beth Ann—can you babysit tonight? Desperate times, desperate texts.

Mom and Dad—who suddenly think Annie is a cyclone—have choir practice. They must've warned all my brothers of my situation, because none of them answer. Not that I ever ask them anyway.

That leaves friends—which, after college, mostly vanished. And Beth Ann. And Elle.

It ends up being Beth Ann and Ryder splitting the shift. I don't know how that deal happened, but I suspect I blew something up earlier and now Ryder is stuck playing basketball with Shane while Beth Ann covers until her late-night inventory shift.

It wouldn't be unreasonable to ask Wally for a raise after three jobs in one day. In most lines of work, maybe it would be. In mine, I honestly don't know what 'normal' even looks like. There's no support group—no circle of frazzled micro-PIs swapping pay scales and hazard stories over burnt coffee.

I don't see the endgame the way Wally does. I never have. I get the middle part—the collecting, the researching, the waiting. The pieces. Not the leverage.

Still, I manage two paid meals today. One is soup—lukewarm, oversalted, but paid for—ordered while I sit alone and let Deedee talk. She isn't underage. She's eighteen. Old enough to skip college, old enough to call a rundown apartment near the beach "freedom."

She seems... fine. Actually, more than fine. Happy.

I don't mention that to Wally. No use giving him ammo.

I get the photo the way he asked—pretending to argue with

my phone, angling the camera, ducking out like I was never there. Like nothing mattered but proof.

And that's the part that clings to me after—the emptiness of it.

Not the job. Not the risk. Not the money.

Just how easy it is to leave the human details behind when no one's paying you to remember them.

But the dinner date with myself?

That's another story entirely.

Chapter −25

When my boss wants something done right, he doesn't ask—he arranges.

Wally sends a black limo. A frigging limo. My neighbors are probably already peering through their curtains, wondering if someone's died and the funeral home sent a hearse, or if I've gone completely batcrap crazy and finally landed a prom date ten years too late.

The chauffeur waits by the back door as I smear on too-red lipstick in the bathroom mirror. The thrifted black dress is sleeveless, ribbed, tight—donated by someone much shorter, so it's not just mini, it's mini-mini. Probably once cost twelve hundred dollars, but I got it for thirty, plus heels that make me feel ten feet tall. I'll stick out like a giraffe lost in a pygmy goat exhibit, but maybe that's the point. I've got so much hairspray in my half-up, waved hair it could double as a helmet. The scent of cheap hairspray hangs around me, sweet and chemical and weirdly comforting.

"Your chariot has arrived, m'lady," Ryder calls from the door, hovering awkwardly. When I look up, his eyes go wide. "Whoa, dude, that's—red."

Did he just call me *dude*?

"Cherry red," I say. "Too much?"

He scrubs a hand through his hair, clearly unsure. "Um, for the car out there and whoever sent it, probably not."

What does that mean?

"Okay, let me reword that—dumb it down—" I start. He narrows his eyes, and I huff a laugh. "Sorry. Didn't know if you were listening. You look dazed. You're a guy—what do you think? Passable? It's a work date thing." I wave a hand down my dress; he looks like he'd rather be anywhere else. He pokes at his cheeks, and I tilt my head.

"Are you okay?"

"Uh. Yeah." He says it dryly, like a joke he's not sure I'll get. "You look just like my dream prom date."

Oh.

Is it that noticeable?

Now I'm stressing, because he's looking at me funny—like I'm not a giraffe after all, but a rhinoceros about to crash through a China shop in a hand-me-down prom dress.

But I have to own it, just like Wally says. "Are you worried about watching the kids? I'll be back in four hours. Maybe five. Dinner's on the stove—grilled cheese and tomato soup. Shane doesn't like soup, so his is the mac and cheese with the hot dog cut into pieces like he's three. He says it reminds him of the lunches I used to make. Annie gets one teaspoon of sugar in her tomato soup—don't ask me why. She'll try to sneak a tablespoon, then barter, then lie about me letting her when I'm gone. Any more than that and she'll turn into a horse, trot across the table. Daisy picks her nose—don't let her. Molly's word of the day is 'anomalous.' She'll think you're a genius if you tell her I can be that way. It means abnormal. I looked it up. She must practice trumpet for at least an hour. Earplugs are on the kitchen counter. My cell phone number is on the fridge. Thank you. I'll pay you when I get paid."

"You don't have to pay me."

"You can pay me," Beth Ann calls, coming up behind him

and letting out a low whistle. "You're coming home tonight, right? 'Cause that looks like an *I'm-gonna-turn-into-a-princess-and-ride-off-into-the-sunset* outfit. You look like a model."

I'm not sure if I should take that as a compliment, considering models are usually atypical. Still, it lands, and my cheeks turn red.

The limo idles at the curb like it took a wrong turn into real life—black paint too clean, windows too dark, engine barely audible beneath the glow of the streetlight and October leaves curling at my feet. Somewhere a dog barks, sharp in the cool air, and the limo's engine hums, velvet-smooth. My porch light glints off the hood, making the whole thing feel staged, as if I'm about to step into someone else's story.

But it really feels good. Even if it is a me-date with myself and it's work. I get to eat something other than mac and cheese or chicken or pizza.

It would all be fine if I could just take some shots of a guy cheating on his wife. But it's not just any guy slipping into that private room at The Gilded Garden—scanning the uncrowded dining area before disappearing inside, a room usually reserved for parties or celebrity guests.

His name is Ray Bernard.

Wally says he's been in quite a bit of trouble for catfishing older women. If that isn't bad enough, I'm pretty sure I know why Wally has me coming here. Not to catch the catfisher. It isn't Ray Bernard at all, it's Renae Michaels, who, per my own research in the limo on the way over, is the wife of a local politician. I would bet Wally needs some sort of information from her and wants to hang it over her head. So, I need to get a picture of her with Ray—in a compromising position.

Normally, everyone would notice her sneaking in the same door. But she slips through a side entrance from the parking lot—the one for celebrity privacy. I watch from my little corner table, alone, surrounded by couples nervously chatting and having their first-date awkwardness. I'm the only single customer, attracting sad stares. One lady even pauses and pats my shoulder as she passes. "You'll find someone, dear."

Ugh. My eyes wander. Sweet smiles. Gentle laughter. The couple to my left: their fingers slide across the table, twining, flirting. Her hand shakes. His eyes never leave hers. When their hands meet, goosebumps ripple up her arm. She laughs, a sound like wind chimes on a porch in spring. He rolls a finger over her wrist, catches her nervousness, and likes it. Imperfectly perfect. I want that. I'm so engrossed—trying not to stare—I don't realize five minutes have passed.

"Oh."

I scoot from my seat, pretending to look for the restroom, then veer the wrong way, feigning confusion. I head straight for the door Ray disappeared through, slip into the dim foyer, and catch them—lips touching. Five photos, quick as a heartbeat, and I'm back out. A waiter intercepts me; I mumble about the restroom. He buys it. I return to my table, eat in silence, and watch the couples come and go.

Later, when the limo drops me back off at home and I've sent the pictures to Wally, who gives me little more than a thumbs-up on my phone, I come back to an immaculate house.

"Did I die on my way home? Am I in heaven?" I call, spinning around theatrically. "Or—oh no—I'm in the wrong house?" The toys are put away, kids are in bed, dishes washed. The house is quiet, except for the TV's glow dancing on Ryder's face as he stands.

He laughs softly. He looks worn out. "How'd it go?"

"Boring?" I admit, stretching out my hands. I've got a massive to-go box the kids won't touch. "I brought leftovers from The Gilded Garden. Hungry?"

"No way. That place is nice. Never been there." He holds his hands up. "But I'm still full from the grilled cheese, and mac and cheese, and hot dogs. That's like gourmet food for me. My fridge is full of stale fast-food takeout." Then, as if he thinks he might offend me, he reaches out and takes the box. "But I can eat more."

"Well, it was overpriced but delicious. I'm not sure they get many single moms there on a budget, because when I asked for a to-go box, there was a general discussion among the staff in the back of the room about what they could put my leftovers in. They kept eyeing me and leaning in like I asked them to fly in a helicopter to pick me up. I honestly think they went out and had a box delivered from the Chinese restaurant down the street just to fill my request."

He laughs, but then I kill the spark in his eyes with something stupid: "Have you ever sat in a room full of people and felt lonely?" It just slips out. I don't know why.

"Yeah, all the time. That's why I asked you out." He shrugs and pulls a slip of paper from his pocket. "Hey, before I forget—Elle said you were poking into some town history?"

It catches me off guard. History? Then my mind snags on the image of that bland little Historical Society card stapled to Jay's notepad. Elle must've remembered it later. Mentioned it in passing.

I take the paper. A name and phone number are written there. **Dolores St. James.**

"Is that the same lady who used to do the litter cleanups at Winslow Park?"

"Used to. Doesn't work there anymore," he says. "She's good friends with my mom. She worked for the old tourism department that covered a few counties, before that new girl came in—"

"Naomi Reynolds."

"Yeah. But Dolores volunteers at the historical society now. Part-time. Hard to catch, but I see her car there early some mornings. She got booted when Naomi came in."

I file it away—Elle never passes anything along by accident—and walk Ryder to the door. I fold the paper and slide it into my pocket, unsure why my chest feels tight about it.

"Thank you again."

I watch him leave, and I can't help thinking of the couple in the restaurant, holding hands, looking into each other's eyes.

"Hey," I call—not too loudly. Ryder glances over the hood as he unlocks his car. "Maybe we can be lonely together sometime, huh?"

He nods—left to right, then up and down—a confusing swirl of yes and no.

The next day, when I stop to pay Beth Ann, she tells me

Ryder already had a date with Hayley Campbell. His second was supposed to be last night, and I kind of wrecked it. Sometimes I think I'm evil, because it doesn't make me unhappy.

Hayley Campbell: thriving real estate, owns a bed and breakfast, toothy smile on a billboard at the edge of town, finger pointing—*Have I Got A Deal For You!*—right above the Chickedy-Dees sign, daring you to fail. Black hair, stunning blue eyes, no kids, rich. Porsche. Two houses, and probably a third somewhere with satin sheets and a wine cellar.

Sometimes I wonder why I only want things out of reach. Or why I keep pushing away the ones I might actually like— afraid they'll end up resenting me for who I am, for what I have, or don't have.

I turn off the lights and head upstairs, thinking about couples holding hands, information passed carefully, and how often the two are connected in this town. Downstairs, the house settles with a sigh, and outside the wind sets the porch chimes shivering.

Chapter –26

Kids lie the cleanest when they think they're protecting someone. By the time Molly bolts for the school doors, I already know she's protecting more than her tardiness.

I drop Molly off last at school, catching her wrist just as she pops the door open.

"Hey—can I ask you something?"

She hesitates, then nods, eyes darting to the hallway beyond.

"Did your dad ever have a computer at the house?"

"I don't know," she says—too quickly. Her gaze skates away, practiced, like she's learned not to finish certain thoughts. "I gotta go. I'm gonna be late for the first bell."

She hops out before I can press, backpack thumping against her spine as she sprints away. I linger a moment, watching her melt into the crowd, filing away the look in her eyes for later.

~

Dolores St. James volunteers at the Pinehaven Historical Society, a Victorian mansion turned museum. I drive past it every morning on my way to the administration office, where I clean. Most days, it's just another pretty building I don't have time for—shuttered half the week, the kind you promise the kids you'll visit when life isn't on fire.

Today, though, Ryder's little slip of paper needles at me— her name, her number, the way he rattled it off like it was nothing. The way Elle must have nudged that info into his orbit, letting it drift over to me like she wasn't orchestrating the whole thing.

A car is parked out front—unusual for this hour.

On a whim, I slow and pull to the curb, my hands making decisions my brain hasn't signed off on yet.

The building isn't open, but when I knock, Dolores lets me in. Instantly, I'm wrapped in the scent of layered history— leather-bound books, dust, aged fabric clinging to its dignity while time chews at the hems. Civil War uniforms stand sentinel along the wall, starch-stiff and solemn. Long tables groan under folders, stacked boxes, and handwritten labels— tiny acts of hope that order can hold chaos at bay.

The quiet inside isn't comforting. It's the kind that makes you lower your voice by instinct, wary of waking something sleeping in the corners.

Dolores fits the place like she was built from the same blueprint—a schoolmarm in her prime, pale cheeks just flirting with wrinkles, red-blonde hair pinned up like she's braced for a day of righting small wrongs. Her clothes say, "I will not be taking nonsense today"—tan slacks, buttoned blouse, sensible shoes. Gold-toned glasses dangle from a chain, and when she smiles, she wiggles them off her face, letting them drop to her robust bosom like a judge setting down a gavel.

"What brings you in here, Misty Dawn?" she asks, savoring my name the way my mother does—like it's a flavor she's still deciding on.

All of Mom's friends call me by my first and middle name, just like she does. When I hear it, I sometimes wonder if Mom wasn't setting me up for a life onstage—or maybe just setting me up, period.

The school bully used to taunt me by that name, like he was auditioning for an MC gig at a strip club. I still haven't figured out if people use it just out of habit or if there's something deeper they all know and I don't.

Maybe it's just repetition.

Maybe it's something they see when they look at me—something I'm still trying to name.

Dolores and Mom both sing in the choir, and every year at the fair they spar for the pumpkin pie crown like it's the Olympics. I'm hoping Dolores won this year. If not, she might take it out on me out of pure principle.

"Can I talk to you about your job at the tourism agency?" I ask, point-blank. If I try to ease into it, I'll overthink myself into silence. "I'll be blunt. I'm trying to find out what Jay was researching before he vanished. He had one of your cards. I can be discreet. I hope you will be too."

Even as I say it, I cringe inside, hearing myself slip into that work-talk voice—too careful, too practiced, pretending I'm just curious while my insides grind like gears. "I'm saying that because nobody else seems to think it's a priority. I have the kids, and they're asking questions."

Dolores nods like none of this surprises her. Like she's been expecting me, and the only question was when I'd finally show up.

"Yes," she says, with a dry little huff. "He joked that if you ever came looking, it'd be because he disappeared. And now... here you are."

I take that in like popping a mystery chocolate into my

mouth—no clue what flavor I'm about to get. The ones with coconut inside make me feel centered and happy, like finding myself on the warm, uncrowded beach as the sun rises.

The ones with peppermint inside, though—sharp and ominous—takes me right back to the time I choked on a candy cane at eight.

There it is. Peppermint.

"Oh, I'm sorry," Dolores says, reading my face, "but you're going to have to hear me rant."

She smiles, but it's resentful, the kind of smile that's been forced into politeness for too long and is tired of pretending it doesn't hate what it hates.

"Because I still hold a grudge," she adds. "And I'm not alone. There's others like me—not just in Pinehaven. We call ourselves the Nine Pins. Like the bowling game—knocked down, replaced, over and over. It started as a joke in a private Facebook group—then it stopped being funny. By the time it leaked into other corners of the social networks, nobody remembered who posted it first."

"Others?" I ask. We sit, and she studies me, measuring whether I can handle the kind of ugly she's about to hand over.

Then she nods once, like she's decided.

"Here," she says. "Let me tell you my story first."

She smooths her sleeve with careful fingers, as if lining up the past so it'll come out straight.

"I worked for the Pinehaven Visitor Bureau for fifteen years," she begins. "Decent pay, endless fundraisers, and a thousand little events to lure people into the parks and, hopefully, the community. Then, two or three years ago, board members started getting swapped out—one by one—replaced by faces from other agencies, newcomers with mysterious grant experience, or kids related to the county's old guard."

She pauses, the silence between us bristling.

"It would happen so fast," she says, "nobody had time to ask why these folks were suddenly taking board positions, or why their family members were suddenly hired to manage the agency."

"And that included Pinehaven Visitor Bureau," I say, feeling it snap into place—like the piece that ruins the picture.

"Yes," she says. "You know it's a small town and most of the board members don't get paid. They are volunteer."

"Like Michael Reynolds—being a county commissioner."

"No," Dolores says, voice sharp as scissors. "He got paid. But after his daughter Naomi got in, he was replaced. Maybe his time ran out—or maybe folks finally saw him for what he was. I never liked the guy. The county was never his top priority."

She leans back, folding her hands. I can see her picking her words—this isn't gossip. It's accusation.

"Step back a bit," she says. "Before Naomi was mysteriously hired—right before he was gone—he was the one who asked for an audit of my bureau. My books were immaculate. We only had lodging taxes, and there aren't that many cottages here. Most of the money went in dribs and drabs to the parks— for managers, cleaning, and trail enforcement."

"Yeah," I say. "I walked them a few weeks ago—a woman got jumped."

"I heard." Dolores's smile is thin, edged. "The local police won't touch the parks. They say they've got better things to do—domestic disputes, paperwork—"

"Sitting up on Jacobson Hollow Road," I add. I've seen them—two cruisers, side by side, trading gossip for hours where they think they're invisible.

"You've seen them too," Dolores says, not bothering to make it a question. She grunts a laugh, but her face hardens. "One day I was there, the next I got a letter from Tyler Maxwell—they were opening a new visitor center in town. Pinehaven Travel and Visitor Center. The Visitor Bureau was now either a private business, no funding, or I had to close—rent and bills coming out of my own pocket."

"The new one's in the old souvenir shop, right?" I ask. "With the 'Explore Pinehaven' sign and the windows painted in cartoon characters for every season?"

Dolores makes a small sound, like she's not sure whether to laugh or cry. "Uh, yeah. I guess you saw the Easter Bunny one."

"The rabbit looked like a green turd with ears," I say—Daisy's voice echoing in my head, flat as a lab report.

That makes Dolores giggle—an actual, surprised giggle that escapes her before she can clamp down on it.

"The one and only," she says. "Wait for Thanksgiving—a turkey with a turd for a wattle."

Her smile vanishes, quick as a blown fuse.

"They made offers to every member of my agency," she says, "scooping them up with the promise of grants handed out like Halloween candy. Bribes, maybe. I know the local winery—and a pet shop with zero connection to tourism—

suddenly had new funding, new signs, glossy brochures."

She leans in, voice dropping, but her eyes dare me to deny it.

"The new tourism department rebranded on social media and started badmouthing me and my bureau," she says. "How poorly the parks were managed, they said. Truth is, we had almost no funding. My income vanished. I was shoved out."

I keep my face blank, but inside I'm boiling—not because small-town pettiness surprises me, but because this scale feels organized.

"For the new department, they hand-picked the board—almost all lodging owners or their kin. Naomi was hired, gets a tidy sum, ten times what I ever saw. Now all the taxes flow into that office and, I suspect, straight back to the same group."

She shakes her head, slow disbelief written all over her face.

"I saw Tyler Maxwell driving a new truck, and he's supposed to be retired," she says. "The part-time park manager quit—no money to run the parks, complaints piling up, and he was getting harassed by the commissioners. So now I'm retired. And here."

"And where does Jay fit in?" I ask. I can feel myself drifting into outrage, and outrage won't find Jay. It'll just exhaust me.

Dolores exhales, her rant sharpening into something more precise.

"He told me he was working on a story for a big newspaper—a piece about the boom in free or low-cost destinations. But every time he poked around, he found these pockets where the tourism offices had been gutted and replaced."

Her fingers tap once against her knee—a nervous tic she probably doesn't even notice.

"He said the new staff barely knew the destinations. They weren't selling the beach or the trails. Just shoving lodging rentals in his face. He said it was more than greed—there was something else."

"A pattern," I murmur—not just small-town corruption.

"Yeah," Dolores says. "It was right about the time he came home to Pinehaven. Said he needed to touch base with home before taking off again. I felt so bad for his kids. He said they were tired of traveling. Needed a break."

My stomach sinks—whenever anyone says the kids needed a break, I picture it: suitcases, motel rooms, a child's voice turning careful, trained by too much moving.

Maybe that's when he decided to drop the kids and run.

I used to think he left the kids for their protection. Now I'm not so sure. He's either dead or hiding, done dragging them from place to place.

Dolores goes on, her voice tightening, the grudge sharpening into something that feels like evidence.

"He came to me, asking how agencies like ours were supposed to work. I laughed—I figured he wanted to write up Pinehaven's booming tourism for his article. That's when I told him I didn't work there anymore. I told him my story, and he seemed to jump on it like a kid finding a dollar on the sidewalk. "

She pauses. In that space, I feel it coming—the shift from her *story* to my *problem*.

"And, well…" Her mouth pulls thin. "He got excited when I mentioned the Nine Pins—people like me, all over the Midwest and South, all booted when Andrew Jones took over as provider for Great Perks Global Reservations. When it was offered to me for the county, I turned it down. It isn't just a reservation system. It's a full visitor management platform set up for each local tourism office—from branding to booking to customer service. Mostly automated. All a small office needs is one person to sit at a desk and smile."

There it is.

"And that would've been perfect for Naomi," I say quietly, "and the others they used as replacements." My chest tightens, the air thickening as the pieces shift.

"I gave him the last known addresses of everyone I knew who'd been fired," Dolores continues, oblivious to the way the name has landed—solid, heavy, like a punch.

Andrew Jones. My mind stops on it.

"Andrew Jones," I repeat, pulling us back to him. "Do you have an address or a phone number?"

She shakes her head. "I only ever saw his name on paperwork. I never met him in person."

He was one of the men in the folders. Not dead. Not vanished. Just a name and a file—until now. And now he has weight. Now he has a role. Provider. Global reservations. Big enough to reach into little towns and rearrange them without ever showing his face.

If there even is one.

I thank Dolores because good manners kick in before I can think, and my hands fidget with the strap of my bag, searching for something useful to do. I tell her if she thinks of anything else to call me, and she nods like she's been waiting years for someone to finally care.

When the door shuts behind me, and I get into my car, something enormous sweeps over me—too big to hold, too sharp to ignore.

A pattern. Just out of reach.

But also... right here, sitting in my palm.

I don't even turn the key. I just sit, gripping my phone, staring through the windshield as if I can glare the world into giving me a clean answer.

Then I text Beth Ann.

Me: *Can you look for info on Andrew Jones, too?*

Beth Ann: *I did. But there's a million men by that name.*

Of course there are.

I choke down panic and force my brain to be useful.

Me: *Focus on travel industry—beaches, Great Perks Travel, reservation systems. Hiker, backpacker, park volunteer. Still alive? Using an alias? Don't let him know we're searching.*

A moment later, my phone lights up.

A thumbs-up.

And the problem with a thumbs-up is that it's the same gesture you give when everything is fine.

Nothing is fine. And whoever Andrew Jones is, he's already been arranging the room long before I walked into it.

Chapter −27

By the time I unlock the side door to the Pinehaven School District office building, my legs ache and my head won't shut up. The kind of day where thinking too much feels dangerous—but not thinking at all feels worse.

I hate sweeping the floors here. But the mindless back-and-forth scrapes the noise out of my head and lets me calm down after a wild morning with the kids.

The building used to be the old brick schoolhouse—kindergarten through twelfth grade, all under one roof. When the new schools went up in the 1980s, everything split into three neat levels, and this place turned into administration. Now it's mostly offices and storage—a dumping ground for every county agency that doesn't know what to do with its old files.

Sweeping takes two mind-numbing hours—back and forth down long halls, into rooms untouched by daylight for years. Shadows gather in corners. Nobody comes around unless they're unloading boxes or ditching paperwork they can't face. The air is thick with the papery tang of old books and dust, sharp enough to prick my nose and sting my eyes if I breathe too deep.

Three floors. The mop is long and ancient, the bottom gummy from years of use. Whenever my thoughts drift, it snags on invisible specks and jerks me forward, nearly gutting myself on the handle. If it slips from my grip, it cracks against the floor, echoing too loud in a building this empty.

And that's where I am after running with Ricky, steeling

myself for my tri-weekly beating from Tina. Sweeping. Thinking.

Morgan Hughes and *John Garcia*—allegedly drowned in the ocean.

Gabe Johnson—dead while duck hunting.

I pull my phone from my pocket and search Gabe's name. The details slide into place, ugly and wrong. He wasn't found in water meant for swimming, but in a drainage ditch near a remote gravel lot. The death certificate first said **POSSIBLE HOMICIDE**, then someone crossed it out. Now: **POSSIBLE SUICIDE**.

He'd been shot in the leg.

The coroner believed it was his own gun—either an accident or a botched attempt to end his life. They said he tried to make it back to his vehicle in the early morning, lost his footing, and tumbled into the ditch.

His gun was never found.

Another man dead near water.

Joseph Taylor, another name on one of Jay's folders, was discovered face down in a deep pool beside an eddy in a creek at a public park. In the grainy news photos, the water looks deep enough to hold a body for a long time, the slow whirl tugging downward, hugging it tight. Long enough to erase evidence when there isn't a bathtub and bleach around. Long enough for someone who knows the land to choose the perfect spot.

Water.

Drowning.

I check my phone again and text Beth Ann.

Me: *Hey, when you get a minute, can you look up drownings in the tri-state region too? Last two years. Especially public places—parks, trails.*

A thumbs-up pops back, followed by a smiling emoji.

Then I text Elle.

Me: *Have you ever set up security cameras outside? Like in a yard?*

I slide my phone back into my pocket and keep sweeping, music humming in my earbuds. Sometimes I drift into a patch of light leaking through a window not blocked by file cabinets or boxes stacked to the ceiling.

I don't hear footsteps on the old stairs.

A shadow stretches up the stairs, slipping into the hallway light at the far end. It reaches my broom first, then my shoes, then swallows my own shadow. I pop out an earbud and step back, leaning to see who it is.

The music leaking from my earbuds gives me away.

"Misty?"

Ryder stands at the top of the stairs. I step fully into the light. "Yeah?"

"Oh. I thought you worked mornings here." He starts down the hall, his limp making his shadow wobble along the wall. He notices, straightens, and forces weight onto one leg to smooth it out.

I must look unsure, because he laughs—awkward. "I had brunch downtown. At the bakery. Wanted to return the favor from the leftovers last night."

He thrusts a box toward me. I lean the broom against the wall and take it, flipping the lid open.

Inside: five chocolate chip muffins. Not just muffins—the *good* ones. The expensive kind they keep behind glass: butter crème filling, dark chocolate mousse on top. I know exactly how much they cost because Molly once stared at them like museum pieces while I bought the marked-down day-olds for the kids.

Eight dollars each. At least.

"Oh no." I snap the lid shut and shove the box back at him. "That's too much. I can't take these."

I tell myself he's just being kind. That I'm putting up walls again. Part of his job is making sure the kids are adjusting.

"You've fed me twice," he says. "Fair's fair." Then he extends his other arm. "And I brought coffee. You get breaks, right? We could talk—without the kids around."

My stomach knots. I glance up the hall and step back, my foot almost drawing a line on the floor, bracing for impact.

"Are we doing this again, Ryder?" My tone's sharper than I mean. "Because I'm not doing anything wrong."

He lifts his hands, all innocence. "Oh—no. Nothing like that. Just wanted to check in. See how they're doing. With their dad still... missing."

There's a glimmer in his eyes—a flash of challenge, just to see if I'll bite. He knows I'm a wildcard. I glare, jaw set, letting a little of my temper show. He answers with a sidelong smirk, pretending it's nothing, but I can see him pocketing it for later. He'll poke at me again, just to watch the sparks.

"I'm not trying to poke the bear," he says, but the grin curling at his mouth says otherwise. It grates on me.

"So, I'm a dangerous bear now?"

He shrugs, half-smiling. "I didn't say that."

He kind of did. I tuck the moment away. Not here. Not now. If I let my temper flare, it becomes another excuse for them to take the kids. I work Wally's tapes in my head—*I choose calm-I choose calm-I choose calm*, over and over, praying it sticks. Sometimes, it just makes things worse.

I don't ask why *he* is doing this instead of the children's services. I don't want to invite anyone else into our lives. And maybe that's the point—space. Observation without any interference.

We sit at a tiny table in an old kindergarten room, surrounded by miniature chairs and faded bulletin boards. Ryder manages to be both professional and a little clumsy— folding and unfolding his hands, his questions careful, voice softer than I expect.

School. Home. Are they settling in? Do they ask about their dad? Have they said anything that might help the police?

That last one slips in smooth enough that I don't notice how easily I answer it.

"Hey, how about this?" Ryder says right before he leaves. "That look on your face when you see me now—" He tosses his head back, rolls a hand through his hair. A nervous thing. He used to do it before a pop quiz. "I wish I weren't the one who made you wear it. I hate it—" He waves a hand like he wants to take that back. "I don't hate your face. That's not what I meant. You hate me; I see it. Don't hate me. I made a mistake. I'm sorry. I should have said that the other day."

I know what he means. I feel it set in. Dread. The recoil. *The uneasy expression. The one that begs it to be anybody else because he's going to have someone take the kids?*

"I don't hate you."

"Yeah, you say that. It's not what your face says. I remember the way you used to look at the principal. He always let Ricky get away with stuff like copying off you and buying the more expensive football uniforms instead of letting that math club you were in go to competitions. You took the blame when he did stupid stuff and called him out on it. But you couldn't do anything, talk back and call Principal Riley an ass, which, by the way he was. Nobody wants to be looked at the way you used to face-shame ol' Riley. What can I do to take it all back, make it right?"

"How about just giving me a heads-up next time if you plan on coming out swinging?" I say. "Like—say something first. Anything."

He nods too fast. "Okay. Yeah. I can do that."

"I mean it," I add. "Not an apology after. Before. One word. Two. I don't care."

He thinks about it, jaw working. His eyes glimpse up to the faded alphabet strip taped crooked above the chalkboard.

"Then let's make it stupid," he says. "So I don't overthink it."

"Of course you want it stupid."

He huffs a breath that might be a laugh. "If I say *yellow light*—that means slow down. Heads-up. Something's coming, but nobody's in trouble yet."

I study him. He's serious. A little pale. Trying not to mess this up.

"And *red light*?" I ask.

"That means stop. Full stop. I'm about to say something you're not going to like. Or someone else is about to."

I tilt my head. "And if I say it?"

"Then I shut up," he says immediately. "No questions. No pushing."

That lands heavier than he probably intends.

"Alright," I say after a beat. "Yellow light, red light."

"Like kindergarten," he says, glancing around the tiny chairs.

"Exactly like kindergarten," I tell him. "Only difference is, if you blow through the red one, I don't sit quietly on the rug."

He smiles then. Small. Real. Relieved.

"Deal," he says.

He hesitates at the door, hand on the frame. "For what it's worth," he adds, quieter, "I don't want to be the reason you make that face. Ever."

I don't soften. I don't reassure him. "Then don't bust through the red lights unless it's an emergency."

And when he leaves, the room feels less crowded than it did before.

After he leaves, I go back to sweeping. Thinking about his smile. The curve of his mouth. The way his eyes hold something back, like he's hiding a secret. I notice freckles on his nose I hadn't seen before.

Just for a second, I let myself drift—

Noah Ryder across a diner table. His hand reaching out. Mine following. Fingers brushing, twining, eyes meeting—

BAM.

I jerk sideways, heart hammering. The mop handle cracks against the floor. No one's there, but my face burns anyway.

Idiot, I tell myself. He's doing his job. He's not flirting. He's not circling back. He's not asking you out.

I lean against a stack of boxes, shaking my head. "Really, Misty," I mutter. "Kids. Laundry. Bills. You fall asleep at the table with your face on the keyboard."

I bend to pick up a box I've knocked over. Papers spill across the linoleum—old forms, reports, folders yellowed and curling at the edges.

And it hits me:

All the county files are here. Just like this box. Tucked away. Forgotten. Holding secrets.

No one ever told me they were off-limits.

Anything truly confidential was supposed to be stored elsewhere. These were what no one thought worth locking up.

Or so I thought. I gather the papers back into the box, hands steady even as my stomach churns.

If the answers are hiding up here, then whoever made people disappear didn't miss this place—they just assumed no one like me would ever look.

Chapter –28

Kids don't wake you in the night unless something is wrong—or something they've been carrying alone has finally gotten too heavy to hold.

Molly woke me just before dawn—bare feet cold on my floor, streaks of tears shining on her cheeks. She said she couldn't lie anymore. Shane had hidden their dad's laptop in the old treehouse behind their house. She made me promise not to tell him she'd ratted him out.

"Maybe it'll help get Dad back," she'd whispered. "Are you mad? Do you want me to give you the trumpet so you can get your money back?"

"No, hon," I whisper. "You're getting too good to stop now. That investment's safe." She's not, not really, but the band director assures me—when I worried Daisy and Annie might go deaf from the trumpet's outbursts—that Molly's right on track with the rest of the beginners. And there's another truth I keep to myself: I'm not sure her dad wants to be found.

Elle shows up around eleven-thirty the following night, boots thunking on the porch, hoodie pulled tight, the faint scent of sawdust clinging to her sleeves. Her coveralls are stained in a way years of scrubbing never fixed—oil, paint, and whatever her work throws at her, each mark stubborn, woven into the fabric like a faded tattoo.

She doesn't ask many questions—just nods when I tell her I want eyes on Jay's place. Not motion lights. Not anything obvious. Just cameras. She swings her backpack around with a crooked grin. "Ricky's always calling me a hoarder for saving these from every house I help gut. Nights like this? Worth it—even if I can't rub it in his face."

By two in the morning, we're running.

Not jogging. Not power-walking. Sprinting—lungs raw, feet smacking pavement. Dogs kick up behind fences, one after another, a chain reaction rolling through the neighborhood like I'd tripped a silent alarm.

No lights flip on.

That's the part that bothers me most.

Twenty-two minutes to cross town. We pause on the sidewalk, hearts pounding. 214 Bayberry Lane. That's Jay's address, and that's where we stand. The neighborhood's hushed except for barking dogs and scraps of wind left by the storm. Clouds hang low, pressing the dark down tight over everything.

"Two," Elle whispers, already scanning the yard, finger stabbing toward the grass. "One *on* the treehouse facing the house. One *inside* the treehouse, watching in case someone comes looking for anything inside there." The computer.

She's a contractor—real-world, hands-on, fixes problems instead of theorizing. There's something grounding about watching her work: measuring sightlines, muttering, climbing like gravity's just another suggestion.

It takes four minutes to climb the ladder with Elle grunting behind me. Two seconds to force open the stiff, warped door of the treehouse Jay built one summer—log cabin style, wedged into the old oak, its limbs thick enough to cradle a house.

My flashlight sweeps the inside.

Molly's old Teddy bears line the shelves, slumped and patient. Comic books. A hoard of empty chip bags and soda cans Shane never threw away. The place smells like wood and childhood memories stuffed in an old cedar chest.

It takes two minutes to retrieve the laptop. Jay's laptop.

Shane hid it in a cubby near the roof, peeling back the wood, sliding it inside, then tacking the board back like he'd learned how by watching Jay. I pull it free with shaking hands.

The first camera goes into the treehouse—tucked high and angled outward, hidden behind the old railing slats. Elle grunts her way around the treehouse, curses under her breath when she bangs a knee, then wedges herself in a corner like she's trying to crawl back out of childhood through sheer will.

"This thing was not built for grown women," she mutters, shifting her weight and knocking into a shelf. A rain of old comic books slides down.

"Jay built it himself," I say. "Which explains a lot."

She snorts. "Yeah. It does."

The second camera she mounts lower, off to the side and on a long limb, disguised in the lingering autumn leaves yet to fall. Anyone cutting across the yard—or going in through the back—will be caught clean.

When she's done, she dusts off her hands and looks at me carefully. "You know, I was Team Misty, don't you?"

Elle is half wedged inside the treehouse, bumping into something, taps one camera, then reaches out for my phone. She scrolls, thumbs fast, already adding an app.

"There." She points the screen at me.

But I'm still stuck on what she said.

"Team *what*?"

She lifts the phone, angling it. "This is the app you use. Look—"

The yard comes into view. Below it, a second window shows us shuffling around the tree like idiots. Me, mouth slack and eyes wide like the ditz I try to avoid people seeing.

"No, I get that," I say, flat. Why does everyone assume I'm such a ditz? I worked hard in high school to stop tilting my head and doing the wide-eyed, blank-smile thing people read as spacey. "What is Team Misty?"

Elle sighs like I'm the one missing the obvious. "It was just a bet. On who Ryder would end up with."

I blink. "What are you talking about?"

"Ricky's always trying to fix him up so we have another couple to hang out with," she says. "Well—and because the pickings are slim around here."

"That's insulting."

She chuckles. "Not you. You're just... inaccessible. You don't orbit the usual circle." She pauses. "Ricky was Team Hayley."

I open my mouth. She throws up a hand. "It's not against you. She's just—she's right up Ryder's alley. The type he usually brings around. Calm. Accessible. Married to work so he doesn't have to get attached and—"

"Beautiful and rich?" I cut in. "And not crazy like this?" I waggle my hands in the air and make a face.

"They're probably in the same tax bracket," Elle admits. She does not deny the crazy. "But he hangs out with us, and we aren't rich and pretty."

"Yeah, you are. Shut up." I glare at her. "Don't un-villainfy yourself. You don't get to pretend you're ugly and poor like I'm such a ditz I won't notice."

She snorts. "We are poor. He teaches at a small town high school. I run my own business in an industry where people still act surprised that I know what I'm doing. And after I do it 110 percent better than the other guy, they still call him to check it." She laughs. "Hayley's nice, but she's got the personality of unbuttered toast. Pleasant. Predictable. Puts you right to sleep." Then she gestures around us. "I'm not sure he'd be into...all this anymore. Not after the fire. Before? Yeah. He was over the edge like you—that's why he worked for the fire department. Not after."

"For your information," I mutter, "I am not *over the edge*. And it's not up to you or Ricky—"

"It's not just us," she says. "It's basically the entire school system and—"

"Stop." I cut her off. "I'm not doing this here. I've got too much going on to hold hands with a guy who thinks I'm shallow."

She looks at me, surprised.

"Ryder chose already," I add.

Elle shrugs. "I just wanted you to know so you didn't hear it from someone else. He's had a major crush on you since middle school. He's got a type, I guess, even when he's trying to convince himself he wants the easy life." She nudges me hard with her elbow. I can't tell if she's joking or not. "You didn't hear that from me."

A *type*. Great. If Ryder's like everybody else, he thinks I'm the stay-at-home mom ditzy type, I think.

She sighs and pokes my phone screen, her eyes hard on me for a second—like she wants to say more, but doesn't. "If someone's watching," she says, "this will tell us."

I nod, pretending I'm calmer than I am. We think we're clear.

We're not.

We're both bent over inside the treehouse when a light snaps on across the street. Elle grabs my shoulder, eyes wide.

A television flickers in a bay window across the street. A door opens. A dog bursts out, sniffing—then freezing.

Its head jerks up.

It charges the tree, barking full throttle, baying like he's got a raccoon treed. I shove the laptop into my backpack just as a flashlight beam cuts upward.

"Misty?"

Marvin Wesley—Mister Wesley—stands there in pajama pants, a coat thrown over his shoulders, the dog straining at the leash he just clamped on its collar.

"It's just me," I call down quickly. "Misty Dawn Bailey." Elle jabs me hard in the rear, like I shouldn't have announced my full name.

I don't flinch. I know exactly what I'm doing. I lean out a little farther, still smiling into the dark. "I'm taking care of Jay's kids."

I grab one of Molly's Teddy bears and hold it up like proof of innocence.

"She woke up crying. Wouldn't stop. Left this here."

The dog snarls. Marvin squints, then waves it off, hauling the dog back.

"Yeah. I know who you are," he says gruffly. "I hear things. Been quieter around here without them."

That's it. No questions. No cops.

I climb down, hugging the bear, and wait—watching Mister Wesley drag his dog back across the yard and into the house— until I can finally give Elle a thumbs-up that it's clear to come down.

I'm exhausted when she shuts the treehouse door behind her, heart still pounding as Elle and I speed-walk back toward our homes. She goes one way down Elm. I cut down Short.

I'm too wired to sleep.

Like Elle said as we peeled out of the neighborhood, "You were grinning like Ricky when he got a tooth pulled last week—high from the laughing gas and goofy."

"Wasn't that fun?" I pump my arm. "Yeah!"

She looked at me like I'd just grown horns, sprouted wings, and flown off like a bat out of hell.

But the rush won't let me go.

I can't sleep, even though I'm exhausted.

At home, I feed two hundred pages—photos from the admin office, records yanked from dusty boxes, screenshots, meeting minutes—one by one into my ancient printer.

The hum rattles the silence.

The pattern starts in Pinehaven.

Dolores St. James had seven thousand dollars in her bureau's coffers—earmarked to pay the part-time park director. It would've put them in the red, but not because of misuse. There just wasn't enough coming in. The commissioners refused to fund the parks.

Refused levies. Refused help.

Letter after letter—Dolores begging for funding.

Every plea stamped DENIED.

Michael Reynolds—Naomi's father—signed the refusals. So did other board members, following his rants about waste and misuse. Meeting notes spell it out plainly: votes cast to let the parks bleed.

Then Tyler Maxwell shows up—loud, vocal, positioning himself as a concerned citizen, hopping onto other boards in the county that had anything to do with decisions affecting the parks. Either no one realized it was a conflict of interest, or nobody cared. Or maybe the ones who did care ended up dead.

Press releases slammed the state of the parks. Social media filled with photos of overturned trash cans, vandalized signs, and ATVs tearing up trails. The timestamps say dawn, but the shadows are long and slanting—late afternoon masquerading as morning.

Some of those dates, I was there. Picnicking. With family.

I don't remember the trash—at least, not like that. Not until after Dolores was gone.

One thing sticks out—a blue recycling bin cropping up in three parks, tipped three different ways. Like someone staged the scene for the camera.

I find newspaper clippings and reports stuffed in a box in an old third-grade classroom. Then newer files—quarterly tax reports from the Pinehaven Travel and Visitor Center.

Over 250,000 dollars coming in every quarter.

Those were recorded.

I wonder what wasn't.

Supposedly, all of it was spent on the director, the building, and "general park maintenance."

Except the numbers never line up.

Digging deeper, I find the hiring records—applications submitted for Dolores's job before she was even gone. Over thirty applicants. The first three are highly qualified. Decades of experience in tourism.

Naomi Reynolds's application isn't even there.

Yet she got the job.

The money pours in. Hundreds of thousands.

But the books don't say where it goes. Just vague categories. General funds. Rounded numbers.

Either Naomi's funneling it somewhere else—or she doesn't know what she's doing.

And that feels intentional.

Jay never connected the dots. He wasn't following a master plan or uncovering some hidden pattern. He just kept chasing—barking up the wrong tree—until whatever he disturbed finally bared its claws. He was more like a little chihuahua after a cat: loud, persistent, convinced he was onto something, right up until the cat stopped, pivoted, and showed him just how much bigger it was.

He thought he was hunting a story. Then the story turned, and suddenly he was the prey. I don't think he ever truly grasped what he'd kicked up—only that it was bigger, smarter, and a hell of a lot meaner than he was. Whatever sent him running didn't fade away. It didn't disappear.

It just waited.

Now its eyes are on me. Jay ran out of road, and the thing he woke is still hungry. He started chasing a story and bolted the moment it turned on him. It didn't stop when he did.

It just changed targets.

I don't get the luxury of running. I have to finish what he started—or be swallowed up, too.

Chapter −29

By morning, the cameras haven't caught anything.

That should've been a relief. Instead, it makes my skin itch.

I sit at the kitchen table with cold coffee and a printer jammed full of half-spat-out paper, watching the camera feeds like they might blink first. The treehouse feed shows nothing but branches swaying and the corner of the yard Jay used to rake obsessively, like neatness might keep the world in line. The side-yard camera catches raccoons. Wind. Leaves scraping along the fence like they're trying to get in.

Nothing human. Nothing moving with intent.

I scroll back through the footage anyway. Once. Twice. Three times. I zoom in on shadows that don't change shape. On light shifts that mean nothing. On empty space where I swear—absolutely sure—someone should've crossed.

Nothing. Which tells me one of two things. Either no one's watching—or whoever is knows exactly where not to stand.

I shut the app and look down at the table, at the mess I made overnight—printouts spread like a bad tarot reading. Numbers circled. Names underlined. Dates stacked so close together they feel intentional. My handwriting grows sharper, angrier, the deeper it goes. I didn't notice when that happened. Only that it did.

There are still two men left on the list from Jay's folders whose fates I haven't tracked down: *Matthew Davis* and *Andrew Jones*. Focus. I start deep dives on them both. I expand my search—up and down the coast, around parks and waterways. I go back one year, then two, then three. Old newspapers. Old social media posts. Then, bam. I find a clue buried deep in an obituary file.

During a high water surge after a storm in April three and a half years ago, Trevor Matthew Davis III, was found without his life jacket near Wilmington along Cape Fear. His boat had been found two weeks earlier—He was an avid boater, and taught boating classes when he wasn't working part-time for Little Pines Tourism Association.

Not the kind of person to forget his life jacket. It was him.

That left one name. The man who signed so many forms— a ghost on paper: Andrew Jones. As I retrace my steps, an ah-ha spark jolts through me. Tyler Maxwell's signature was on a few forms too—grants, meeting notes.

I pull them up and compare them.

The handwriting is almost identical. My ghost, Andrew Jones, hasn't vanished at all—he's just been using a different name.

The kids are still asleep. The house creaks the way it always does when it's deciding whether to settle or give up entirely. Somewhere in the walls, the heat clicks on, then off again, like it's unsure it wants to help.

I gather the papers into stacks—Dolores, Reynolds, Maxwell, the new tourism office—and stop when I realize something small and stupid and dangerous.

Every one of these decisions was made in daylight. Public meetings. Recorded votes. Signed letters. Nothing hidden. Nothing illegal enough to trip a wire. Whatever took Jay didn't need secrecy. That's when my phone buzzes. Not a call. A notification. *One of the cameras detected movement.*

Chapter −30

I waited until Elle and Beth Ann were here before I opened the clip.

The house is loud with kids—some thudding soccer balls in the backyard, others burrowed into the couch and on pillows on the floor, transfixed by a movie. For the first time today, no one's tugging at me or calling my name. The hush feels rare, precious.

I take advantage of it.

I slip out my phone, its smudged screen catching the overhead light.

"Look," I say. Both of them lean in, elbows nudging the table, eyes bright with curiosity.

The treehouse feed flickers to life—a static shot of the door, two button-eyed Teddy bears perched on the shelf above like silent sentries. Everything's exactly as it was: no movement, no shift. A hush hangs there, the kind that clings to places after kids have outgrown them.

I swipe to the side-yard camera. Fence line. A patch of churned mud by the old oak. The narrow strip of earth, always shaded, slick with last night's dew.

"Oh, look there," I murmur, voice barely above a breath.

That's when it appears.

Not someone moving through the frame. Someone standing, motionless. Just at the edge—too far back to trip the camera the usual way. Half a shoulder. A hint of a sleeve. Dark fabric that seems to absorb the night, not reflect it.

The figure doesn't move. They wait—patient, deliberate.

I scrub back ten seconds. Elle and Beth Ann freeze, breath held. The figure vanishes.

"Gone," Beth Ann murmurs.

I jump ahead twenty seconds. Empty frame.

I scrub again, slower, frame by frame. My stomach swoops—when the pattern finally snapped into focus.

They never entered the yard.

They leaned in. Testing the line. Testing me. They knew exactly where the camera stopped—and stood there.

Close enough to brush the camera's limit. Close enough to know exactly where it failed. Whoever it was—no accident. They wanted to be seen.

To let me know they could.

I set the phone down, hands tingling. "Whoever it is knows I'm watching," I say. "Feels like a game of hide and seek, but I'm not the one doing the counting. Someone else is and cheating, peering out between their fingers. Watching."

Neither of them laughs. The kitchen holds its breath, too.

"I honestly believe Jay wanted me to find this," I add, dragging his battered laptop across the table. I type in the same password Jay used for everything—the old house address. The screen glows. I catch their gazes before I go on.

"I found a pattern—drownings, all linked to men in those folders I pulled. Last night, I found another—Matthew Davis. Cape Fear, boating. *Allegedly*. I asked Beth Ann to dig deeper. She found two more—a child, and a woman who drowned in a hotel pool. Nida Sanders. Just a few months ago."

Beth Ann nods once.

"Last night, I couldn't sleep. I watched the cameras, dug

through Jay's laptop, sure I was chasing ghosts. Folder after folder—buildings, city streets, strangers' faces."

I pause, remembering it.

"I opened a second folder. Same thing. Then a third. A fourth. A fifth. Hundreds of bland images. None of the kids, which I expected." I look around, make sure the kids can't hear, and drop my voice. "Jay was never about them."

I swallow.

"But then, three hundred images deep, I found her—red hair, unmistakable. The same woman Jay was with at the Old Driftwood Bar and Grill."

Elle and Beth Ann move closer behind me. Beth Ann leans in when I tap the screen.

"Your doppelgänger," Beth Ann murmurs. "That's...odd."

I click the photo open. "Remember the picture I showed you from the bar? Same woman."

"That's the Capital Cove Regency Hotel," Elle blurts, finger jabbing the screen. "Ten, twelve stories? Big golf complex. Ricky and I blew our anniversary budget there—offices up top, fancy rooms down below."

She grins at our stares. "We splurged. Sometimes you just have to."

She pantomimes a golf swing, lips pursed in a cartoon "Pftttooo," following her invisible ball into the living room. All three of us glance over at the chaos: kids sprawled across the couch and floor.

"Glad you had a blast," I deadpan, rolling my eyes. "Last vacation I had? Spring break, college—Myrtle Beach. Not exactly the Ritz." I tap my temple. "Owoo."

"Well, if you'd gone out with Ryder, he would've taken you somewhere nice," Elle says with a shrug. "He's loaded."

"That ship sailed," Beth Ann laughs. "She had a date—mystery guy, limo, the works. Ryder's with Hayley Campbell tonight. Another date."

I catch myself shooting Beth Ann a look—somewhere between jealous and annoyed, though I barely register it. She must notice. Jealous? Please. Not me. Especially not over Ryder and Hayley. Still, there's something squirming in my chest, a pressure tightening between my ribs and stomach, like I've lost something I'll never get back.

"Hey, I'm Team Misty," she says quickly as if that fixes it.

"My date was a business dinner," I mutter. "Is there a newsletter about my life I don't know about?"

Between Dolores and Marvin Wesley—whose dog treed me last night—I'm basically an open book. There's no more whispering in corners. Everything's out loud, in Technicolor.

"And he can date whoever he likes," I say. "We don't need to pair off to survive. I don't need a man telling me what to do."

I hear the edge in my voice and wince. Their pity stings. I'm turning into Marvin Wesley—grumbling, pacing, TV flickering blue at two a.m.

"That's not what my man does," Elle says, eyebrows waggling like she's auditioning for a cartoon.

"Please, spare me," I say, hand up. "I run with him every morning. He belts out love songs with that ridiculous grin. I don't need a mental movie of what you two do behind closed doors every time he jabbers and I say 'uh-huh.'"

"He wuvs me," Elle coos, pressing a fist to her chest.

Between that and her biceps, Beth Ann and I both laugh despite ourselves.

I sigh and turn back to the laptop. "Enough. This matters. You two binge too much reality TV—I'm not your drama fix. I live in the real world, where people actually get murdered."

I drag the photo into the browser and wait, pulse tapping in my throat. I know what I'm looking for. They don't.

Same face. Red hair sharp as a warning. Eyes flat, unreadable. She pops up at least sixteen times—same hair, same haunted stare.

"Her name was Rae Jean—Nida Sanders," I say softly. "Friends called her R.J."

I pull up the obituary. Then the photo from the bar.

Beth Ann draws in a sharp breath. "She drowned. Hotel pool. Alone. At night. There's a note. Names the hotel."

Capital Cove Regency Hotel.

"Everywhere Jay went, death followed," I say softly. "And now it's at my door."

Elle straightens, jaw set. "I'm bringing the kids in."

And not one of us argued. The air feels colder now.

Chapter −31

Tyler Maxwell always wears button-up shirts and khaki pants—short sleeves in the summer, long in the winter. Whenever he gets excited, he does this funny, lopsided dance, like a movie pirate with a wooden leg.

When he steps out of the bank on Tuesday, he's doing that swagger, a smug grin stretched across his face.

Just like every day this week.

I watch from my car, parked less than a block away.

I'm ready to tail him.

The only drawback is that Noah Ryder walks past, seemingly oblivious—then turns when he notices my car.

He doesn't bother knocking.

He just opens my door and slides in.

Wonderful. Exactly what I needed. Frustration bubbles up, tightening my chest.

"Well, just come on in," I mutter, sarcasm dripping from every word. "Uninvited."

"Ouch. Were those muffins really that bad?"

"No, they were actually good. Thanks." I drum my fingers on the steering wheel, trying not to watch Tyler Maxwell slide into his own car. "But I've got things to do, places to go, people to see."

I jab a finger at the business Ryder just exited.

The sign over the door: *Campbell's Tri-State Realty— Hayley Campbell.*

"Is this a red light, then? Your girlfriend might punch me

in the face if she sees you in here with me."

"No, yellow. And Hayley's not like that. She's not hotheaded like you. She would not punch somebody."

Ryder taps the dashboard, fingers drumming a little rhythm.

I twist in my seat and glare at him.

"I'm not hotheaded."

"Yeah, you are. You punched the crap out of me at recess in third grade." He yawns, hand cupped over his mouth. "And she knows where we stand. I told her you turned me down before I ever asked her out."

"Whoa, now." I throw both hands up between us.

He pretends to flinch, eyes wide, like I'm about to swing.

"Is that what this is all about? All of this with the kids— some kind of payback because I punched you in third grade?"

I pause, searching his face for a crack in his act.

"Do you remember *why* I punched you, Ryder?"

"Because you're hotheaded."

"No. Because you kept poking my nose and chanting, 'Poke the bear, *poke the bear.*'"

I reach over and tap the tip of his nose, just like old times.

"You would not stop."

"Because you got mad in class, grabbed Ricky's pencil, and snapped it in half." He waggles his hands beside his head, pulling a face. "And went all crazy. I was trying to save your life. He would've killed you. I saw his eyes when you were heading for the slide. He had plans."

"I can't believe you're bringing it up. Third-grade hijinks."

I inhale, scanning the dash cubby for my tapes.

My gaze lands on the worn tape: *Calm Yourself. Discipline Your Anger.*

I can hear it in my head already.

I choose to feel calm.

It isn't working. Not even close.

I need that sultry cassette voice actually telling me what to do.

"The reason I broke the pencil was because he kept poking my back and shoving my chair. Mrs. Pendleton got mad at *me* for asking him to stop."

I choose to feel calm.

You are calm.

No, I'm not.

"She yelled at you because you screamed at him and kicked his chair. And I gave him that pencil for his birthday. It had a Green Rider comic book series eraser on it. I got it from the bubble gum machine, and it took like fifty tries."

"Oh my gosh. We're doing this, aren't we? Talking third grade like we're nine years old."

This is madness.

My jaw aches from clenching. My eyes ache too, stretched wide with anger. Everything feels too hot—like I might snap.

"Get out."

"No," he says simply.

"Give me that tape over there—" I point a finger toward the cubby. He scoffs, but reaches in and starts to latch onto *Be a Warrior. Be Strong.*

"Nope. Not that one. You really would regret me listening to that one right now."

I lunge across the seat and snatch the calming tape.

I wish I didn't need this.

But I'm going to explode if I don't.

I shove the tape into the cassette player and fire up the ignition so it'll play. I put the car in drive, hoping he takes the hint. I keep my foot hard on the brake so the vehicle doesn't inch forward.

"What's that?"

"My calming tape."

I jab the cassette player, willing it to work faster.

"Because right now, I kind of want to kill you." I hiss. "And this tape is the only thing stopping me."

Gentle music drifts from the speakers. That syrupy voice begins, purring that I'm in control of how I feel.

I'm not feeling it. At all. The irritation is still buzzing, sharper than before.

I am in control of how I feel, I repeat beneath my breath.

Then, grinding my teeth:

"Why are you doing this?" I ask.

"Because I know what you're about to do, and I can't let it happen."

I narrow my eyes, studying him.

"You know what, exactly?"

He knows—*what?*

I crank the tape's volume, drowning him out.

"I know I'm going to poke the bear."

He actually does it—reaches out and taps my nose.

My hands ball into fists.

Right before I snap, I crank the volume all the way up.

"Because once again, I've got to step in and save your butt."

"My butt does not need saving."

"I AM IN CONTROL OF HOW I FEEL," the voice booms, relentless and chipper.

I inhale as his finger taps my nose again.

"I AM IN CONTROL OF HOW I FEEL!" I shriek back, voice cracking.

Ryder's eyes jerk wide.

There's a slight smile on his lips, like this is deeply satisfying to him.

"I CHOOSE TO FEEL CALM," the tape insists.

"Poke the bear," he whispers.

He taps my nose. Again.

"STOP," I snarl.

"I CHOOSE TO FEEL CALM," the tape chimes again, oblivious.

And this goes on—him tapping my nose, me screeching— until my hair stands on end, skin buzzing.

I slap my hands over my ears the way Annie did before her legendary three-year-old meltdowns.

Hoarse, I finally twist to face him, the steering wheel digging into my ribs.

"WHY ARE YOU DOING THIS?" I yell, hands flailing wildly. "Just stop! Please stop!"

I'm right on the edge of angry tears—which almost never

happens.

That's when I catch the glint of my pepper spray in my purse.

Granted, I was only going to use it for show—not actually spray him—

—but Ryder's gaze drops.

He sees what I'm thinking.

I see him register it.

He goes pale.

He sinks back.

For the first time, he actually looks like he understands what he's been doing.

Right as I'm screaming at him.

I reach for the purse.

He moves at the same time.

"BECAUSE," he yells, face beet red, "I DON'T WANT YOU TO GET YOURSELF KILLED LIKE BILLY DID! YOU'RE JUST LIKE HIM!"

My hands freeze mid-air.

"Right now," he shouts, "you're sitting on a barrel of gunpowder, giving off sparks—and you don't even care."

I lean too far.

My foot slips off the brake pedal.

The car lurches forward.

Boom.

We slam into a fire hydrant—a bone-jarring jolt—and only stop when the hydrant wedges under my front bumper. Water explodes into the air, drenching the car and everyone nearby.

People scatter, shrieking and laughing like they've stumbled into a street fair instead of a disaster.

"Boom," Ryder mutters.

I turn to him, my heart lodged somewhere in my throat. "I think that yellow—" I snap my fingers, trying to find it. "—went straight to a red-light moment." I wince. "But this one's on me."

Wow. I hate admitting that.

He just stares back at me, then throws his hands upward in a silent blast, fingers flaring wide before fluttering down—mimicking fireworks raining out of a split barrel.

All I can do is turn forward and watch the water cascade over my hood, stunned and silent, as the street keeps moving like nothing just cracked open.

Chapter −32

"So how long have you known I'm looking into Jay?"

My voice comes out careful. Measured. I'm not even sure Ryder suspects anything—or if he's just a pro at reading wreckage as it rolls by, cataloguing every dent.

After my SUV got towed to Don's Automotive so Big Don could snap my bumper back into place, Ryder ended up here with me at The Pines Diner. "Just in case," he said, which I took to mean: in case the job dragged out and I missed school pickup. But really, I think he just didn't want to leave me alone.

I feel deflated. Not defeated—just... leaking. Like a party balloon with a slow leak, air sneaking out until you're left wrinkled and sinking. The kind of tired you feel in your bones, down to the marrow.

Never thought it'd be Noah Ryder—the guy whose core personality used to revolve around poking my temper like a man prodding a hornet's nest with a short stick, just to see what would happen—keeping me grounded today.

But here we are.

He drove me so I didn't have to ride with Big Don, who has a rugged—and I'm being generous—scent about him. I couldn't stay in Don's waiting room anyway. It backs right up to the garage bay, and the smell of oil and rubber makes my skin crawl. I hate it during oil changes. An hour and a half would've finished me off.

I'm still waiting for my mom to call and ask how I managed to ram a fire hydrant in town. Curious passersby watched me, wide-eyed, as if I'd just chugged a gallon of espresso and started talking to fire hydrants. One of them was the choir director—legendary for passing along gossip to my mom before I even got home.

"That you were looking into Jay's disappearance?" Ryder asks. "It's a no-brainer, Misty. Anybody in your orbit knows you don't let things go. And the kids aren't stupid. They know you left the other night. They saw their dad's computer."

His arms fold. "You're playing a dangerous game."

The Pines Diner is stubbornly stuck in the 1950s—chrome polished to a mirror shine, red vinyl booths patched and re-patched, still sighing when you sit. The jukebox hums in the corner, amber light honeying the air. The scent of frying bacon and burnt toast clings to every surface, making it greasy, familiar, safe.

The server drops off coffee. I take a sip—bitter enough to make my eyes water, the taste scraping down my throat like charcoal.

"It tastes like they started brewing it back when Reagan was in office." I note, then sigh. "I don't have a choice, Ryder." My fingers curl around the chipped mug, grounding me. "Jay didn't just stack the deck against me—he got up and left the table. I'm the one still sitting there, no cards left, no way out."

"Walk away," he says. "Let the police handle it. I'm giving that yellow light right now."

I bark out a laugh. "Yeah? How's that working for me so far?" The bitterness in my voice almost matches the coffee.

He goes quiet, hands shoved in his pockets.

"I'm not Billy," I add. "If you're looking for redemption,

find someone else to save."

He huffs a laugh—but his face doesn't match it. "I can't do that, Misty."

He doesn't look at me at first. Then he does.

"I'm not looking for salvation. I'm just—" He exhales. "You're killing me, alright? Since that stupid punch in third grade, I was all in."

"What?"

"You're like a drug," he says, shrugging. "Or a demon. Or something. You got into my soul and I can't get you out. Ricky thinks I'm crazy."

He worries his lip, then pushes a hand around his cup. "I said too much."

I stare at him. Speechless, which never happens.

A stupid smile tugs at my mouth before I can stop it.

"You're laughing," he mutters. "Great."

"Flattered," I say. "Honestly? Honored."

"Oh. Even better."

"I mean," I add, nudging his hand where it curls around his coffee mug, "you *are* Noah Ryder. I saw in the paper you got voted most sought-after bachelor at that charity auction. Raised a few thousand for the Humane Society."

He groans, face flushing. "Mabel Evans won. She's ninety-two. Her kids pooled money as a joke."

"I bet," I say—and this time, I'm smiling on purpose. I wiggle my fingers toward the little creamers in a bowl by his elbow. "Can you pass me like six of those? This coffee tastes like mud. I need to tone it down to muck."

"You're going to have to fight me for them," he says, reaching for the bowl. "I think they made your coffee before mine. Mine's at least sixty years old."

I don't know why I think he actually means it. I feel like the wrinkled, shriveled remains of that now completely deflated balloon.

I lunge, stretching across the table and nearly spilling both coffees to snatch a handful of creamers from under his fingers. He's startled—he didn't expect it—but jumps in, competitive as ever. Our hands tangle for a second, both of us stubborn, neither letting go.

I'm half-standing, half-falling, and then I burst out laughing—loud and unfiltered, a snorting chortle that ricochets off the chrome and vinyl.

"Wow," he says.

I realize I'm gripping the creamers so tightly a couple of them burst, cold streaks down my fingers. But that's not what he's talking about when he finally lets go.

He's looking at me, noting my laugh.

"See?" I giggle. "I know how to break the spell. Mom says men like sweet, self-possessed voices, gentle as a dulcimer and as melodious as a Wood Thrush's call."

"Yeah, that was pretty much the opposite—more like the unrestrained, maniacal cackle of a hyena."

For a heartbeat, I'm not chased, or cornered, or braced for the next hit. I just sit there, breathless and laughing, letting the moment exist.

Then my phone buzzes.

Big Don, calling to say my SUV's done.

And whatever that moment was—fragile, messy, perfect or not—gets snapped by real life yanking us back into motion.

I sigh, already annoyed at the timing, at the interruption—until I realize I don't actually want to get up yet. And that's new. That part makes me uneasy.

I gather my things, my usual urge to bolt already kicking in—and Ryder stands up like it's assumed. No question. No hesitation. Which is annoying. And...unsettling.

Because it feels right.

There's got to be something about a guy who hears a laugh like mine and doesn't bolt. Maybe that's what makes him worth sticking around for.

Chapter −33

When I came home tonight, my foot caught on something as I wiped it across the welcome mat.

White.

I stop, look down. A corner of paper sticking out where it doesn't belong.

I nudge it with the toe of my shoe, then bend and lift the mat just enough to wiggle it free. For a split second, I think it's a church flyer—one of those bulletins from the creepy place out by the highway that keeps trying to save souls that aren't asking.

It isn't.

It's from my mother's church.

The paper is folded once, careful. Deliberate. I turn it over, and on the blank back side, someone has written in neat, practiced handwriting—letters shaped the way people do when they've had years to perfect not being noticed.

I don't want to make trouble, but I saw a man walking around your house this afternoon.

He had a windbreaker hoodie pulled up and kept his face turned away from the street.

He looked in the windows.

He drove a truck and parked it down the block where I couldn't see the plates.

You may already know this, but I thought you should.

—E.J.

I stand there longer than I should, the paper light in my

hands, the porch suddenly too quiet.

Edna Jefferson never makes trouble.

And she doesn't write notes unless she's watched long enough to be sure.

I snap my head to the right and catch her curtain moving—just a twitch, the smallest give of fabric, like she realizes a second too late that I might look up.

Chapter −34

I've noticed Shane growing quieter. The change isn't loud—it thrums beneath the surface, a hush in the corners of the house, a pause stretched before his answers. He used to pretend to bounce an imaginary ball, launching it toward a phantom hoop. Yesterday, for the first time, he didn't do it. Not once. I grew up with five brothers—each wired differently—but if any of them suddenly dropped a habit, it was always a warning sign. None of us, though, ever had a missing dad.

At first, I blame pressure—school, basketball, homework piling up faster than he can keep up. For months, he lived out of hotel rooms, evenings swallowed by the blue glow of his phone or numbed by the TV. I can picture him snapping at Daisy and Molly when their laughter cut too loud. No one told him to call it a night. No one hovered over math worksheets. No parent in the stands, no coach barking at him to hustle. Just the low hum of a hotel fridge and a silence that seeped into everything—a hollow, waiting quiet.

No wonder the transition stings.

Every day, I try to reach him. "How was school?"

"It was good."

"Ready for your game Friday?"

"I'm starting. Coach Rick has me on varsity again."

I want to celebrate, to shout it from the kitchen. But there's a trace of something in his eyes—tightness, a shadow of guilt, or maybe something darker—and before I can say more, he vanishes to his room, door clicking softly behind him. I'm left holding the silence, wondering if I missed the moment he stopped trusting me.

Still, the worry sticks. Molly, too—she pulled out an English test, C circled in red, wide-eyed for my reaction before shoving it into her black binder. She hasn't worn the new lipstick and eyeliner I splurged on, either.

Maybe this is just what teenagers do.

Withdraw. Pull inward.

Saturday morning bites through the windows, kitchen tiles icy beneath my bare feet. I spread everything across the table—notes, files, a mug of coffee cooling to sludge. The plan is simple: lay it all out for Pinehaven's Chief of Police, Daniel Mercer, and let him take it from here.

My hands shake as I stack the folders. The sunlight on the table looks too bright, too clean for everything I've dragged out of the dark. I've gone as far as I can alone. Government data—criminal records, sealed reports, deep financials—is locked tight. I can't pull phone pings or vehicle logs. I can't set foot on Tyler Maxwell's property or in his house without a warrant. Every path forward slams shut, cold and metallic, authority closing in like a cell door.

But there's one more thing—one path left—and it needs someone who works outside those lines. The only name remaining tied to a ghost.

Beth Ann knows everyone in Pinehaven. She's the kind of person you trust with secrets you don't even realize you're spilling. She knows them like a seasoned cashier—by habit, not rumor. By what people buy and when. She can spot the biweekly paychecks in the mid-month rush. She marks the parents by the bulk cereal and stain remover, the pet owners by the cat litter they claim is "just for a friend." She notices the ones who hover in the candy aisle, who dodge her gaze at checkout, who pick up the expensive soap only when life is going well.

She knows who works nights by the hour they wander in. She clocks who's stretched thin by the brand of toilet paper they quietly swap for something cheaper, who grabs the discount deodorant with a practiced shrug, pretending nothing's changed.

Beth Ann spots the hidden threads everyone else misses.

So, when I tell her what I need—a signature that's clean, public, and something Tyler Maxwell won't question—she nods, no questions, already plotting.

She tells him she's collecting signatures to start a cat shelter in town, her smile bright and harmless as sunlight on linoleum. Not money. Not donations. Just support.

It sounds harmless. Civic. The kind of thing you feel like a jerk turning down—especially with ten people shuffling behind you, leaning in, reading over your shoulder, silently judging what kind of person you are.

Tyler hesitates, pen hovering midair, his jaw working. Just long enough for Beth Ann to clock the uncertainty.

Then he scrawls his name, the motion quick, almost careless. He pauses just long enough to glance up at the security camera over the register, then presses down harder as he signs.

Beth Ann thanks him, her smile never wavering, and slides the paper away with practiced ease, like it's nothing.

But when she hands it to me later, her eyes meet mine—a quick, sharp exchange. There's something beneath her smile now—a warning, or maybe pride.

The handwriting curls the same way, pressure darting in familiar places—the same impatient jabs I've seen on invoices signed by Andrew Jones, the supposed owner tied to every Great Perks office that funneled money where it didn't belong.

The name doesn't match.

The handwriting does.

Perfectly.

I sit with that realization too long, letting it settle in my bones, heavy as winter air. For a breathless second, I almost wish it wasn't true—because if it is, then every risk, every secret, every night I spent pretending things were fine, was just me playing a part in someone else's escape.

Either Andrew Jones never existed—or he was never the one holding the pen.

Suddenly, the list of names on my table feels unfinished— like the story's changed shape while I wasn't looking.

I spread Jay's files out again—not the evidence, but the bones of it, the way he built his fortress. Pages thin as onion skin, every piece arranged to keep his hands clean.

How he moved. What he insulated. What he didn't.

Jay documented risk obsessively. Every name had context. Every meeting was buffered—burner numbers, indirect asks, layers on layers meant to keep eyes sliding past him, never landing.

Except in one place.

Me.

There are no notes about shielding the person who'd step in if he vanished. No instructions to slow things down. No warning about visibility.

Because he didn't want that.

If someone was going to be seen, it couldn't be him.

The realization settles—heavy, sharp, leaving a bitter taste at the back of my throat.

Jay didn't miscalculate. He offloaded.

He turned himself into the absence and made me the presence.

When the fight was about to start, he passed me his sword like it was nothing—like a plastic toy you'd hand a kid on Halloween: bright, harmless, meant to look dangerous, never meant to draw blood.

I take it without thinking. Lift it. Wait for him to finish whatever he's doing—tie a shoe, catch his breath, step back into place.

When I look up, he's already gone.

Moving in the opposite direction of the fight as the first blows land.

Leaving me gripping something useless, the room suddenly colder. I stand there a beat too long, staring, my thoughts scrambling for any explanation that doesn't shatter the world.

I'm five again in the grocery store, reaching for my dad's hand without looking—because it's always there.

Except this time, my fingers close around something unfamiliar. Too cold. Too big. Not his.

I look up, and it's a stranger. And for a heartbeat, I forget how to breathe.

Chapter −35

I don't look at the signature right away.

I set it on the table with the rest of the paperwork and walk off like it's nothing. Make coffee. Rinse a mug. Let the house creak and settle around me. I've learned the hard way that if something is going to change the shape of things, you don't rush it. Take a break. Come back and look it over. Again and again and again.

Wally may think that collecting data and information for him is all I do and all I learned from him. It's not. I've still got that old police experience they drilled into my head for nearly four years. I realize then that maybe having Annie wasn't why I left. Maybe it was because a lower-level police officer at Pinehaven—the place I would always sit because I had a kid and was a woman—was not enough for me, not enough to keep me busy. They just steadied traffic, stopped the domestic disputes and guarded bodies, held crisis at bay until the detectives rushed in to finish the quest.

The quest—the pursuit of the crime and the criminal and the part I found exciting.

And now, I've always latched on to it like a puppy gnawing on a bone. I feel like this is what I'm made for.

When I come back, I spread everything out again.

Invoices from Bennigan's Harbor Tourism Center. Funding requests from James Cove CVB. Maintenance reimbursements from Little Fear Bay Visitor Center. Different offices. Different letterhead. Different reasons.

But the same pattern.

Each one routes money through a separate intermediary—companies with names bland enough to slide past notice. Bittle-Dyson Reservation Services. Jane Cameron Software Support. Shells with just enough paperwork to look legitimate and just enough activity to keep them alive.

I line them up.

The amounts aren't large on their own. That's the trick. Five thousand here. Twelve there. Twenty routed through "software updates." Small enough to avoid audits. Frequent enough to add up.

And then I follow where they land.

Not scattered. Not diversified.

One account.

Same bank: Offshore Alliance Bank. Same branch: Offshore Alliance—Littleton Branch. Same routing number. Always the same final stop.

I sit back slowly, the chair creaking under my weight.

That's when I pick up the signature.

I don't need a forensic expert. I don't need magnification or software. I've stared at these documents long enough that the handwriting lives in my head. The curls hit the same way. The pressure spikes in the same places. The impatient jab at the end of the last name—the tell he never bothered to fix.

Andrew Jones signed the paperwork.

Tyler Maxwell signed the paper in front of witnesses.

Different names.

Same hand.

The room feels smaller all at once, like the walls leaned in while I wasn't looking.

This is proof.

No guesswork. No theory. A straight line you can trace with your finger: money leaves public offices, passes through polite little companies no one questions, and lands exactly where Tyler Maxwell can reach it.

He'd found the perfect place to hide out in Pinehaven—a bland wannabe tourist destination begging to be a part of the Atlantic Coast shoreline, asking no questions because they felt entitled to it.

And make a bit of money off it.

I lower the paper back onto the table.

This isn't a mystery anymore.

It's a funnel.

And now that I can see it, I know something else too.

Whoever's been careful all this time never bothered to hide this part from me.

Because if someone was going to be visible—it wasn't supposed to be him.

Chapter −36

Sunlight slants across the kitchen floor, dust motes spinning in the glow. It takes me half the afternoon to let my wall down and make the call—a simple act that feels colossal.

For the first time all day, I'm out of everyone's orbit, the silence sharp and private. I don't know why I'm nervous. I don't think Ryder's out to get me anymore—he's had plenty of chances if he were. But this isn't official, and it isn't casual either. I need someone off the books. Beth Ann's at work. Elle's driving the boys to games, and I know her speaker's on in the car, and her kids know my kids.

I pace the kitchen—once, twice—the phone a weight in my hand. My heel finds Nacho's tail, and he hiss-screeches, offended. I scoop him up, his fur warm and ticklish under my chin, murmuring apologies as if he understands the stakes. He blinks at me, unconvinced. I hit call before I can talk myself out of it.

"Misty?" Ryder answers on the second ring, his voice crisp and awake—like he's been waiting for trouble to find him by phone. "Hey," I say. My voice sounds steadier than I feel. "I've got a green-light moment here."

There's a pause. Not long—but real.

"Okay," he says. "Talk."

"Shane and Molly are acting strange. Quiet. Slipping off. Not where they're supposed to be when they're supposed to be there." The hallway stretches away, shadows pooling in corners, as if it's keeping secrets too. "Nothing dramatic. That's what worries me." I'm terrified Jay's got something to do with this.

The kids haven't asked me to find him in weeks.

They used to ask every day.

Another pause, the kind that buzzes. I catch muffled sounds on his end—keys clinking, a chair scraping, the hush of someone standing up. Something is shifting, invisible but certain. "I'm on my way," he says.

"I didn't ask you to—"

"I know," he cuts in, gentle but firm. "Green light. You called before it got loud."

"Hey, I'm asking you off the record. Not work. I would ask my brothers, but—I've got to be honest, Ryder, my family supports me. Supports us. But everybody thinks I'm setting myself up for a fail—"

I close my eyes. That lands harder than it should.

"Ten minutes," he adds. "Don't do anything until I get there."

"I wasn't planning to," I lie.

"I know," he says again, like he's learning me in real time. "That's why I'm coming. You got this."

You got this. He has no idea what that does to me—how just those words feel like being wrapped in a blanket, warm from the dryer. No one's ever told me that before. Ever. But hearing it, even if I'm not sure I believe it, makes me think maybe I can.

When I hang up, the house exhales into a hush—quiet, but restless. Like the walls themselves are bracing for news. I don't know what I'm afraid of finding. I just know I don't want to find it alone.

~

I slap together some fried chicken for supper, moving on habit and muscle, the kind of cooking you do when your head's full and your hands need something simple to follow. I'm already backtracking—wishing I hadn't called Ryder—and at the same time, relieved I've got backup. Both things can be true. They usually are.

"Hey," I call toward the living room, keeping it casual. "Ryder's coming for supper."

Molly's gaze darts up from the couch, sharp and immediate, then flits away. She tucks her knees under her chin, pretending the movie demands her full attention. Her expression is unreadable—a lock without a key. That's when Shane comes out of his room.

Not slow. Not reluctant.

He moves like he's already decided something.

He springs once off the floor, taps the doorframe—a ritual from childhood I haven't seen in months. He ducks his head, but not fast enough to hide the grin pulling at his mouth. Not a smile.

A grin you wear when you've pulled something off — and nobody's caught you yet.

"Everything okay?" I ask, keeping my voice light.

"Yeah," he says too fast. "Just... hungry."

He grabs a plate, still grinning at nothing, and for a second it hits me wrong—not because he's happy, but because he's contained. Like he's holding something back on purpose.

The kind of happiness that doesn't want company.

The kind that thinks it's funny I didn't see it happen.

I turn back to the stove, oil popping softly, and tell myself not to jump at shadows.

But the house feels different now—a little too alert, as if the walls themselves are leaning in to catch our secrets.

When Ryder arrives, he's all casual, as if this is something we do all the time—even though it's not. We gather around the table, laughter skipping from Annie to Daisy and back. The weight in my chest eases, replaced by a flush of embarrassment. I feel like I've yanked the alarm bell and there's no emergency—just the echo of my own nerves. Now I'm sure Ryder thinks I'm angling for a date, inventing trouble just to see him.

Ryder shoots hoops with Shane and Molly for an hour. Their laughter drifts through the window while I scrub shampoo into the younger kids' hair, the air steamed and scented with lavender soap. When the house quiets down again, dusk has crept in, and the kids trail inside with cheeks flushed from the cold.

After Molly and Shane disappear into their rooms, teeth brushed and voices hushed, I pull on my sweater and walk Ryder out to his car. The air outside is sharp, full of autumn and woodsmoke. "I swear, they have not been acting like that all week," I tell him, glancing back at the house. I catch a face at the window—gone before Ryder's eyes can follow my gaze.

"They give me, what, eighteen hours of training for this?" Ryder says, half a laugh in his voice. "But there's nothing in the manual about kids whose dads are missing and presumed dead." He stuffs his hands in his hoodie pocket, breath ghosting in the night air. "Shane's more restless than usual. Molly keeps her guard up."

I know why. He's good-looking, and Molly's thirteen—old enough to notice, young enough to act like she doesn't. She's lucky she doesn't have brothers like mine, who would've spotted it immediately and made a sport out of pointing out every awkward tell, turning it into a running joke the way they always did with me.

"I can give you some therapist names if you think they need help dealing with grief or abandonment or whatever they must feel right now." He reaches out and pokes my arm. "But they are hardly deserted. They have you. And they've mentioned that before. You're the constant in their lives—the one stable thing they've probably ever had."

I pull my sweater tighter, fingers curled in the sleeves, the scent of fried chicken and cold night clinging to the fabric.

"I feel ridiculous for asking you to come over," I say, laughing under my breath. "They put on a whole show."

"Well, that I think is a cue that shouldn't be overlooked," he says. "We can keep an eye on them. Ricky said Shane has seemed off at school. He's been watching out for him, too. You know you've got a whole community here, right?" He makes a circle with his finger. "Your instincts, so I hear, are spot on."

"So you hear?" I ask. What does that mean?

"That's just what I hear." Around? From who?

He laughs softly. "Hey—the chicken was amazing. Thanks for supper. Not that I'm hoping the kids are going to have nervous breakdowns, but I'd be more than happy to check on them a few times a week just to eat something that isn't fast food." He stops short, like he's been punched in the gut by his own words. "I could cook too. I'm not saying that...oh, hell.

You'd think I'd never talked to a woman before when I'm around you."

I let him stand there in it.

"You're not like anybody I've ever met," Ryder says, softer. "You've got it all figured out—or it looks that way. I'm just not loaded like Jay. Not some hotshot reporter, risking his neck and making bank."

"What? Loaded?"

"Your mom told Dolores, who told my mom, that you like guys who are loaded." He laughs.

Oh. Mom.

Heat flashes up my neck, my face going all the wrong shades.

"You're good."

"I work for the county. Yeah, I got a settlement from the fire, but—"

Please don't make me explain this. I shift on the gravel, wishing the ground would swallow me.

"*Ripped*," I mumble. "That's what my mom meant. Five years ago, my brothers roasted me because I glanced at a guy running shirtless in Winslow Park. I looked—what else was I supposed to do? But they acted like I'd clubbed him and dragged him back to my cave. They called him 'the ripped guy' for months. My mom didn't like the word—she got it in her head it meant something worse, so now she calls it 'loaded' instead."

He chews on that, then bursts out laughing—bent double, shoulders shaking, like I've just told the best joke in the world. He wipes his eyes, then, without thinking, wiggles his fingers at me. Without thinking, my hand finds his fingers warm against mine. *Oh, my gosh, are we having a moment?* My belly jumps. This is not normal for me—

"Why is that so funny?" I ask.

"Because it's the first time you've really let me in," he says, still laughing. "I thought you'd just admit you like rich guys, but you drop a whole saga on me instead—"

Then, just like that, he sobers—his hand still wrapped around mine. "You've got this," he says, voice steady, eyes searching mine. Serious as hell. Then he lets go.

He's still laughing as he stumbles to his car, wiping his eyes, his breath fogging the glass. He rolls down the window, grin wide, eyes bright in the porchlight.

"I guess I'll have to start working out harder, huh?" he calls, his voice curling with mischief. "Maybe I'll come run with you and Ricky."

Chapter −37

It isn't until Saturday night, sometime after eight, while I'm getting ready to do one last check over of my paperwork headed for the police station on Monday, that I notice how the quiet in the house has changed—thicker, pressing at the edges. And that the huge folder I had tucked into what I thought was a safe place was missing.

At first, I thought I had misplaced them.

Daisy and Annie are in the living room, shrieking with laughter, smacking each other with couch pillows. Their noise is normal—background chaos, the soundtrack of a house still holding together. A storm looms on the horizon, I feel it in the pressure on my sinuses. A bit of thunder shakes the house and both girls stop and pretend like they are scared, jumping under blankets and giggling.

But what's absent isn't just the folders of evidence. It was Shane—his voice, the way he'd bark at his sisters, the thud of his footsteps overhead.

He usually yells at them to knock it off when he's trying to watch something. Sharp, irritated, loud enough to rattle the window glass and remind everyone he exists.

I don't hear him.

Molly hasn't wandered through for cookies or chips—a ritual as steady as sunrise. I haven't heard the blare of her trumpet slamming my ears.

I glance at the clock. An hour. Or was it two? Too long. I look up, suddenly aware of how deep I've been in the paperwork. Shane's door is closed. I knock. Nothing.

I knock again, harder this time, then push it open, already telling myself I'll feel stupid in a second. The bed is untouched.

Sheets folded back the way they were this morning, like he just jumped out of it and never came back. No shoes. No backpack. No phone glow under the covers.

A chill crawls down my back, sharp and immediate.

I move faster now—down the hall, to Molly's room. Her bed is empty too. The blankets are still neat. Her trumpet lies against the pillow, unopened case, exactly where she left it.

I stand there a beat too long, staring, my thoughts scrambling for any explanation that doesn't crack the world clean in half. Then I'm moving. Feet pounding the hallway. Heart in my throat. Where would they go?

I stop in the kitchen, hands shaking as I snatch up my phone. I open the security camera app and pull up the backyard feed at Jay's house in real time.

I scrub the footage back.

Back again.

And there they are.

Two shapes slipping across the yard—careful, familiar. Not running. Moving the way you do when you believe you've timed everything just right. The way kids move when they think they're invisible.

My heart starts pounding hard enough to blur the edges of the screen. I freeze the frame. And in the far corner—right where it stood before, just beyond the camera's clean line— there's something else.

Not a blur. Not a trick of shadow. A figure. Still. Standing exactly where the camera fails. The same distance back. The same angle. The same refusal to step forward. It doesn't follow them. It doesn't hurry.

It waits.

That's when it hits me—not as fear, but as certainty.

This isn't someone watching *the house*.

This is someone watching *them*.

And they already knew which way the kids would go.

Chapter −38

My gaze darts to the living room. Daisy and Annie are still laughing, jumping up and down on the couch now with the blanket over their heads as if the world hasn't cracked open behind them.

I make myself focus. Panicking, overthinking—that's how people die. I grab my keys and shove my phone into my pocket. I look into the other room at Daisy and Annie.

I can't bring them with me.

I peer through the front window.

Across the street, a curtain stirs. Just a breath of movement—deliberate, not accidental.

Edna. Sunday school teacher. Junior high English, retired before I ever made it to middle school. President of the garden club. The kind of woman who catalogs the world quietly, tucking details away like pressed flowers.

She's safer than leaving them alone. Safer than buckling them in and driving straight into whatever's waiting out there.

Let Pinehaven gossip. I don't care if they hear her side before I've even shut my car door.

I pound on Edna Jefferson's screen door—hard enough to rattle the frame. Annie grips my left hand, digging in her heels. "Why can't we just stay home?" she demands, her voice flat with suspicion. Daisy, who's already let go, steps closer and nudges Annie's shoulder. "Come on, Annie. It's just for a little while," she says, voice soft and steady, the way you talk to wild animals. Annie scowls, tugging harder at my hand. "We never get to do anything fun when you get that voice." Daisy just shrugs, her eyes already scanning the porch like she's memorizing the way out. Both of them stare up at me—one daring, one resigned, both waiting for an answer I can't give.

She opens it like she's been waiting for us all along.

"I need you to take the girls," I say, Annie still squirming at my side. "Please." No explanation. No preamble. "Just for a little while."

Her eyes dart past me—toward my house, the yard, the dark swelling at the edge of the street. She doesn't ask questions.

"Would you girls like to come in and have some cookies and milk? I baked them for my cooking club podcast, but it would be fun to try them out—" Edna only nods and steps aside, silent and certain. Daisy nudges Annie, who gives me one last glare, then scoots inside.

As the girls disappear down the hall, the scent of freshly baked cookies drifts out. I breathe it in—a warm, buttery calm that feels impossibly safe next to what waits outside. Behind me, the storm gathers, thunder muttering and the smell of rain-soaked pavement sweeping in through the door. I slip one of the envelopes—one with the return address still printed in the corner—into Edna's hand. Across it, I've scrawled in blocky pen: *If I'm not back in an hour, call the police. 214 Bayberry Lane, Pinehaven.*

Chapter −39

I turn off the headlights when I'm two streets away.

Old habit. I don't even realize I'm doing it until my hand reaches for the switch and stops halfway there. The dash lights glow softly, painting my knuckles blue. The road is empty—the kind of hush Pinehaven only gets when every porch light is off and everyone else is tucked in, convinced nothing bad ever happens this late. The silence presses in.

I park a block up. Gravel crunches under the tires—a sound that always feels louder at night, like it's echoing off closed houses. My pulse bumps in my fingertips as I kill the lights.

Not in front of the house. Not even across from it. I nose the car in beside a line of bare-limbed maples and kill the engine, letting the cooling metal tick in the hush. I linger, hands locked around the wheel, listening for any sound out of place—dog bark, screen door, the whisper of gravel under a shoe.

Nothing. That's worse.

I pull my hood up and step out, easing the door shut until it barely clicks. I reach back in for the pepper spray from the glove box, and the Louisville Slugger I keep wedged under the seat. The air is wet with the scent of rain-soaked leaves, cold dirt, and a faint whiff of wood smoke. Down the block, a porch light blinks on, then off again, like someone changed their mind about seeing anything. I move on, shoulders prickling.

I don't take the sidewalk.

I cut through yards I've never crossed, slipping between hedges and fences, keeping to the deepest shadows. Jay's house crouches dark at the end of the street—empty, abandoned, pretending to be harmless, its windows blank as bored eyes.

The back of it is worse.

No lights. No movement. The kind of stillness that makes the air feel held, as if someone already passed by and even the crickets dared not break the hush.

I pause at the fence, count to five, then vault it quietly, landing soft in the grass.

Then the worry creeps in. All the what-ifs my mom drilled into me before I left for college, alone for the first time, dart through my mind. The speculations and future-gazing for safety—habits ingrained by the police academy—surface, unbidden, like old ghosts of warning. If I call the police, I'll have to explain myself right here and now when stealth is to my advantage. So instead, I text Ryder: "Red Light. Jay's house." Sent. I regret it instantly. Too late. If I waited for backup, the kids might be dead before headlights hit this street.

The back door is right where I remember it. The handle is still loose. The frame is still warped just enough that you have to lift and pull at the same time.

I ease it open inch by inch.

The house exhales.

A wave of closed-up air rolls out—dust, stale air, something faintly spoiled leaking from the refrigerator. I slip inside and leave the door cracked. Not shut. Never shut. I stand still, letting my eyes adjust, heart thudding too loud in my chest.

Through the kitchen, I can see into the dining room.

Beyond that, the living room. Shadows move there. More than one.

"—don't. They're my kids. You can't. I'm not—just let us go. You've got your money."

Jay's voice. Alive. The realization lands flat, strangely dull. No rush of relief. No gratitude. Just a sharp irritation creeping in, unwelcome but familiar.

"Seriously, Jay? You thought you could just wave a folder and make this all go away? That's not how it works. All you've done is put a neon sign on the trail—right to my doorstep. And you know what? Trails like that, they never disappear. Someone always comes sniffing."

My folder, I presume. I can picture Jay telling Shane that if he just handed over everything I'd collected, he could fix it all—save his dad, save everyone. That's what that smile was tonight, what all his dodging meant this week. He wanted to be his dad's hero.

The voice continues, calm and almost bored. "You know I can't let you go. You'd run straight to the authorities. Why the hell'd you bring your kids, huh? I don't want to hurt kids—but you brought them here. Got them involved."

A hard stomp, the sound of a heel slamming down.

"That human-shield trick of yours might've helped before. You already tried that on me. But now they know something's wrong. They've seen me. So, here's what's going to happen. In about ten seconds, I'm going to shoot you. Then I'm going to shoot your kids. Then I'm going to put the gun in your hand and make it look like you did it."

Tyler Maxwell. Movie logic—lazy, brutal, confident. And if

he had enough time, he could still make it look like anything. But Molly's sobbing guts me. I pray he's the kind of man who can't bring himself to hurt a crying little girl. The trail behind him was mostly men, almost all caught off guard. None of them had time to beg or cry.

The sound of his voice makes my stomach heave. I expected him. I didn't expect *this*. Still, I can't say I'm blindsided—just furious at myself for ever thinking this would end neatly. That I'd stroll into the police station Monday morning, lay the evidence on the chief's desk, and walk out while the cuffs went on Tyler's wrists with a line of police officers on each end of the hallway clapping their hands as I walked down the middle. My hand in the air in a fist like a victor.

He's a pillar of the community. Every man who died because of him probably bought into the same polished lie. Tourism agencies from here to Ohio have handed him awards, thrown grant money his way, churned out press releases fawning over his "vision." Jay, on the other hand, just looks like a deadbeat dad—someone who'd abandon his kids, maybe even shove them under a bus if it meant saving himself.

I shift my weight, careful, grateful this isn't my old house with its groans and creaks. Jay's wall-to-wall carpet—even in the kitchen—feels like a blessing. I slide forward, hugging the shadows until I can see the back of Tyler's head. Gray-brown hair, mussed like he's been grinding his hand through it. His arm moves, the pistol visible now as it angles toward Jay. It's a pocket pistol, small enough for close work—meant for bodies, not distance.

Is he bluffing? He's trembling, his whole body quaking from head to toe.

The answer hits me clean and cold.

He doesn't want to do it.

He's not the killer. He's the signer. The funnel. The man who moved money and paid others to be brutal so he didn't have to be. A cornered mouse pretending to be the cat.

So, who *was* the cat?

The back screen door squeaks behind me.

Padded footsteps. Close. Too close. My shoulders go taut, my stomach jittering as if stuffed with marbles.

"You're realizing how stupid this was right about now, aren't you?"

Oh. No. Wally. Wally's voice is deep and satisfied at my back.

I turn my head slowly, the scene in the living room fading to background noise. A gun presses cold against my skull. He shifts to keep it there.

Wally—a hardened, retired city cop who's seen his share of death—and gotten numb to it. I know. He's told me stories that made me shiver, hands clamped over my ears.

Wally. Who almost got me killed at Winslow Park. Who nearly had me shot at Myrtle Beach. Who knew exactly how to stay just out of sight. Who warned me off Jay's case before I ever asked. Who had information ready before questions were even formed? Oh, my— that day in the dollar store, when Beth Ann realized I did private investigative work. It all clicked into place. George Goodson hadn't been searching for me by accident. In fact, he hadn't been searching for me at all. Someone had sent him my way.

Wally. No. Oh. Yes.

"Hotheaded, ditzy gingers like you don't get jobs like this to catch the bad guys," he says, almost conversational. "You're a distraction. Something shiny for the idiots to chase." He lifts his free hand, and makes air quotes. "You think I hired you because you're skilled?" He snickers. "No, after I scrounged you out of the dumpster, the only reason I kept you around was to babysit the kids that were the bait to lure your boyfriend back."

I'm stunned. "*Ex*-boyfriend," I mumble. Like it is notable.

I'm going to die right here like the others. Except I have something Wally doesn't—maternal instincts and the knack for thinking on my feet in any emergency.

Raising four kids will do that—teach you to improvise when panic isn't an option. Like pulling together a science fair project at nine o'clock the night before. Chasing off a neighbor's feral dog with a lawn chair before it bites a leg. Like dodging bake sales that you can't afford.

Ditzy ginger, my ass. Let them try keeping up with four kids and a mortgage and a mother who texts me every morning to ask if I'm eating enough protein. I'd like to see them last a week.

I go from shocked to furious in less than two seconds— quicker than Wally expects. I'd bet good money he's wishing he'd kept his cash instead of paying for those lessons with Tina. Or for that *Warrior* tape that's played in my head night after night while I vent frustration, burning it down into muscle on the punching bag in my garage. Suddenly, it's all there.

I've been working on my roundhouse kick. The pivot. The

way you bring your leg up and arc it around. Tina taught me to aim for the hip—because it's dirty to hit anywhere else.

But tonight is all about dirty.

I whip my foot up and drive it hard into Wally's crotch. He folds forward with a strangled sound, all air leaving him at once. As he keels, I snap the baseball bat up and smash it into the hand holding the gun. It flies free, skittering across the room.

I don't stop moving.

I wheel around and bring the bat down again, cracking it against the side of his head.

Wally collapses to the floor. I don't know if he's out. I don't wait to find out.

Normally, this is where I'd run. That's how it usually goes with Tina Metzger. I land one good hit—one solid, surprising shot—and then I bolt. Because that's pretty much all the moves I have. And she always tells me she can and will kick my butt if she catches me.

She's right. She can.

But there's nowhere to run tonight. No bell. No mat. No coach barking corrections while I gasp for breath—and she smiles like she hasn't even broken a sweat. Just a gun behind me and a man who finally stopped underestimating me a second too late and right now, is probably wishing he didn't. And irate that he did. So I don't run.

I lunge for the gun, slip, go down hard, and come up with it clenched in my fist just as Tyler turns toward me, his own weapon swinging in my direction.

The room spins.

I know how to use a pistol. I used to hit the range in the police academy every day. But I'm a bit rusty. Haven't held one since I quit. I've never shot anyone. Never wanted to. But he's here. And I'm here. And I can see Jay herding the kids out the open front door—and of course, Jay goes with them.

That's it, Jay. Abandon me again, you coward.

And there's no space left for wanting when Tyler turns— and I hear Wally scrambling up behind me. This isn't about Jay. Not now. It never really was. It's about the kids.

I aim. Feet spread, arms low—just like I did more than a couple times as a cop. I shift, both men in my sightline now. I'm past trembling. Shane and Molly's lives depend on me holding these two off until they can get to safety. I picture their dad shoving them behind him, tripping over himself in his scramble to get to the car first. And that makes me furious.

I don't calculate. I don't think about what comes after. I do what anyone does when the math collapses, and all that's left is instinct and bone-deep refusal. I go for the scared one holding the gun first.

"Tyler, drop the gun or I'll shoot. I've shot men before, and nothing will stop me now unless you drop it." I lie. He doesn't know that. Rumor in Pinehaven always had it that I left the force after shooting a guy who kicked his dog. Small town drama, small town gossip. Today, it works for me—just like it did when Wally hired me and I never corrected the record. My voice is deeper, steadier than it should be. Years of Mean Mommy Voice, honed across dinner table fights and morning battles over alarms Shane 'forgot' to set so he could sleep in an extra hour and miss school.

"And you, Wally, hit the floor. Yes, I'm hotheaded. And yes, every time you've called me Ginger these last three years has made me a little crazy. I've bottled it up to keep my job. I'm like a soda shaken on a hot day—about to burst. Pop."

I think Tyler's going to shoot as I swing my aim back to him. His finger tightens on the trigger, but at the last second he flings his arms up, and the bullet rips into the ceiling.

The blast is deafening—too loud, too close. My ears ring. Plaster dust rains down. The tang of burned powder floods my nose, stinging and sharp, and for a split second I think he's hit Wally, who suddenly bolts for the back door, legs jerking like a startled deer.

Tyler reels back, more startled than hurt, his shot wild—into the ceiling, into nothing. Wally stumbles behind me, swearing, crashing into a chair instead of me.

And then—Sirens. Edna. She didn't wait the hour.

Not distant. Not maybe. Real. Close. Coming fast.

Red and blue light strobes through the front windows, washing the walls in color, breaking the spell of the room like glass shattering. Tires scream outside. Doors slam. Voices shout commands that don't belong to any of us.

I freeze where I am—half on the floor, gun heavy and all wrong in my hand, heart battering my ribs, wild and frantic.

Jay is already gone. The kids are alone. Figures.

Hands grab my shoulders—firm, controlled, not rough. Someone pries the gun from my fingers. Another voice is yelling at Tyler to get down, to drop it, to not even think about it.

I don't argue. I don't explain. I just sit there, shaking, the noise finally crashing over me, the weight of everything pressing down all at once.

Somewhere outside, the night air is split by the smell of rain and distant barbecue—hushpuppies, and collard greens—Pinehaven's lingering after-dinner perfume, Carolina-style.

The world keeps spinning, but inside, my hands won't stop shaking.

All I can think is: Pinehaven's a little bit safer tonight because of me. And two other broke moms that nearly everyone underestimated.

Chapter −40

"Telling me red light five minutes before shots are fired does not count."

Ryder burst through the door two minutes later. He'd caught Shane, who was three steps off the front walkway. Shane turned and realized his dad had come out behind him—with Molly.

"Okay, next time I'll ask the idiot who is shooting to give me a time frame."

He's staring at me, head tipped like he wants to ask if there's going to be a next time—and the thought clearly terrifies him.

I was standing there shaking, handing the officer the gun—lungs burning. My shoulders drop. "I knew you'd have my back, Ryder," I say. "It just took a second to realize it." Then I jab a thumb to the door where Jay went out. "Because that's what I'm used to alright? Baby came back through one door, then went out the other." I smile a little, let the waves of relief start passing over. "Guess I'm never getting that moment either."

"Hey," he pokes my shoulder. "I'm standing right here. You're getting it right now. I'm just not the drama kid like Bobby, but if you really want me to scream it out loud—just walk out that door."

I didn't.

One cop told me later he'd never forget the look on Shane's face when his eyes shot up to his father—shock first, then something sharper. Outrage. Shane shoved him back with both hands, screaming for him to go help me. Again. And again.

Then the shot went off.

Shane bolted, trying to get past his dad. If Ryder hadn't caught him around the waist and hauled him down, Molly right behind him, he would've run straight back into the house.

There were only three officers on scene at first. They were busy with Wally Singer and Tyler Maxwell—both in handcuffs and being escorted to the police cruisers.

Jay jogged to his car and drove away.

Gone again.

~

Five days later, Ryder stood at the far edge of my backyard, arms spread wide like a referee preparing for chaos.

"Okay," he said. "We're going to go slow, because I'm not convinced you all understand the concept of red light, green light. Or at least Misty doesn't."

I stood with the kids on the opposite side of the lawn—not just Shane, Molly, Daisy, and Annie, but Ricky's kids, Elle's kids, and Beth Ann's too.

The adults cheered from the fire pit, balancing frozen pizza boxes and skewers of half-burnt marshmallows. It was cold. Annie complained loudly and continuously.

"Green means go," Ryder called. "Red means stop. Yellow means—"

"Baby steps!" everyone shouted.

It had become a standing joke.

Sometimes he threw in yellow just to watch us shuffle forward in exaggerated caution, like we were daring each other to trust the ground.

Shane always won. He was fast. He cheated when he thought he could get away with it. And considering everything, he was taking his dad's disappearance outwardly better than anyone expected.

All three kids were rolling with it.

So was I.

~

The original files went to the police the next morning. Once I handed them over, I couldn't take them back. Not copies. Not summaries. The real ones.

Wally Singer and Tyler Maxwell were arrested within the week—quietly, without press or spectacle. Pinehaven doesn't like attention when it turns out everyone missed something obvious.

Wally hadn't been chasing criminals.

He'd been managing them.

Jay Hensley vanished again. This time, no one pretended it was temporary.

~

As the night wore on, my front lawn filled up—kids running, laughter echoing, the smell of smoke and sugar in the air. At the edge of the yard, the sign leaned a little to the left. Ryder and I had argued about whether it mattered. It didn't.

THREE BROKE MOMS DETECTIVE AGENCY.

While I was prying wood from the garage rafters, I glanced at Ryder. "So, I've heard I'm your type," I teased. "What's that mean—red hair? Slightly unhinged?" I waved my hands by my head, mimicking the move Ryder made before I hit the fire hydrant.

He sniffed and looked away—kind of cute, actually. "No, my type's always been a hot-headed, smart girl who never backs down from a fight. The red hair and freckles are just a bonus. It's the whole package."

"Why'd you never ask her out in high school?" I asked, pretending I didn't know he meant me.

He shrugged. "The problem was, I was never the type that hot-headed, smart girl wanted."

"Maybe you are. You just don't know it."

"How would I know?"

So I kissed him—quick, surprised, like neither of us had planned it, and neither of us needed to apologize.

Later, Ryder called out, "Red light," and everyone froze mid-step.

Even me.

For the first time in a long while, nothing was chasing us.

And that felt like enough.

www.ingramcontent.com/pod-product-compliance
Lightning Source LLC
Chambersburg PA
CBHW070917180626
46817CB00003B/1102